Canela

Carmen Lezeth Suarez

To Teresa.
Faith. Family. Elvis. Guesthouses. Pool boys.
And always, *LOVE*.

Acknowledgements

I wanted to try and thank everybody. I started listing names. Page after page, I realized this could be an entire book in and of itself. So simply, thank you to all those who helped me become the woman I am today. You know who you are. And you know I got mad love for you.

Tomatoes.

Although this book is based on my personal experiences, names and places have been changed, moments amplified or downplayed, others completely omitted. In a lot of ways, this is a work of fiction. Please do not miss the LESSON for the trees. Everyone in this story is a reflection of someone who actually changed my life in all the ways that ultimately mattered. This is my story. And this is how I chose to tell it.

The beginning…

I wasn't like everyone else. I was the Black kid, the Latin kid, the kinda White kid. More times than not, the nigger kid. The poor kid, the parent-less kid, the family-less kid. The one with no home, no place to go. The dumb one. The kid who couldn't read too well or too fast, who couldn't put two words together without stuttering. I struggled with school, with my apparent "otherness"—all the time trying to figure out why people thought of me the way they did. The Black kids didn't think I was Black enough, the White kids thought I was surely not White enough, and the Spanish kids talked too fast and knew too much Spanishy things for me to always understand. Now, I don't remember much of my childhood, but amongst all the chatter in my head there was always a calmness, maybe a clarity, when I heard my mother's voice. No matter how confused, scared, or engrossed in thought I was, watching my mother, being near her, hearing her words, gave me comfort, a quiet strength that would follow me for years to come.

Emma

When I was little, I remember running home from school after being called names by some older neighborhood bullies. Mama saw the tears streaming down my face and the fear in my eyes and, to stop me from shaking, she grabbed me and hugged me hard. She kissed me on the forehead. Not something she ever really did on a regular basis. She wasn't a touchy-feely person after all. I was young, maybe six or seven years old at the time. I held on so tight; finally she pulled me away. Kneeling before me as she wiped my tears, she asked me what was wrong. Through my huffed breaths and salty tears I asked, "Why do the White kids call me nigger and why do the Black kids call me spic? Why does everyone hate me so much?" I couldn't catch my breath. Mama gently put one hand on my chest as if to magically slow my breath. I calmed down.

As I sniffled along, she pulled up the right sleeve of my shirt and then pulled up her own. She put our forearms side by side. My arm was so tiny next to hers. We were the same exact color. And in her story-telling voice, all in Spanish, she said, "You're the color everyone wants to be. The color of cinnamon. In the summer they lie on the beach and want to be the color that God blessed you with. You've been kissed by the sun. That's why they hate you. It's jealously." She smiled and almost laughed as she spoke, she knew this problem all too well, "They'll always call you names, Carmencita, some good and some bad, but you should never pay attention. And they will do it over and over again and you can never take it to heart. Never be afraid Carmencita." She then gently tapped on my chest with her finger. "Promise me you'll always remember, even if I'm not with you, I'm always right here, in your heart, you just have to listen closely. Okay?" She winked at me and continued on, "Only listen to people who actually know who you really are inside and love you anyways." I looked up, not fully understanding what she meant, but I kept looking into her big brown eyes. She was now re-braiding one of my pigtails, holding an elastic on the side of her mouth. "This color, this beautiful cinnamon, is one gift God gave you. It's not the most important. It's not more important than the legs He gave you to walk, or the arms He gave you to help, or the brain He gave you to think." She lifted up my arm again and kissed it gently. "But this skin color is a gift and never let anyone tell you who you are. No matter what anyone says, okay?" I nodded up and down.

This was my first lesson in race relations and probably the most significant one in self-esteem. Mama would always repeat those lines to me throughout our brief time together so they stuck in my head pretty fiercely. I used to sometimes roll my eyes when I was a little older because I'd heard it so much. But now—now I understand its importance.

Those are the things I remember about Mama. I vaguely recall what she looked like but I know she wasn't a big woman—not too fat, not too skinny. She was a mother-shaped mother. She seemed really tall and giant-like to me, but I realize now that was because I was so little when she died. Her hair was brown, short and feathery-like; now when I think back on it, I guess it was probably thinning. I do remember specifically my mother's great smile. She didn't smile often, but when she did, it was from ear to ear.

She also had that happy gleam in her eyes. Whether she was happy or sad, there was a brightness about her that always made me feel like I was going to be okay. When I was alone in the bathroom sometimes, I used to look in the mirror to see if my eyes did the same thing. Twinkle. When she would walk by and catch me staring at myself, she'd yell at me to stop it! She'd remind me that it wasn't good to be conceited. I didn't really know what that meant at the time, but I knew it must be a bad thing, so that stuck in my head forever too. "It's not good to be conceited."

***

I thought about you. A lot. I wondered if parts of me looked like you. My straight nose, my smooth curly hair, my small brown eyes, my high cheekbones? Truth is, other than my cinnamon colored skin, I didn't look like Mama at all. I certainly never had her twinkle.

11

I wondered why things were the way they were, but I just didn't know any different. Mama was all I had. She was all I'd ever known. So to me, this was my normal. And I loved Mama. She taught me so many things in our short time together, things I've never forgotten, and moments that stayed with me forever and eventually...saved my life.

* * *

I don't remember much, but what I do remember is vivid, like it just happened yesterday.

It would be past eleven at night and I'd run into my mother's room when she'd come home from work. I'd sit at the other end of the bed and watch as she'd put her short hair in little rollers. She'd clean her glasses with a tissue and I'd see her calloused and seemingly rough hands. Her fingers always looked as if she'd stayed in the bathtub too long. I knew it was from all the cleaning she did. Mama was a housekeeper back then. Like clockwork, she'd put cream on her hands and then she'd turned on the television and start watching the news. My eyelids would be so heavy and, without even looking my way, she'd remind me that I should be in bed. But I couldn't help it... I'd struggle to stay awake if only to spend a little time with Mama.

You know, she worked so much. She was a housekeeper for two different families. And sometimes, when she could get the work, she also worked as a teacher's aide at the local school. But mostly she worked as a housekeeper for rich folk so I never got to see her except in the early mornings before school. She didn't seem to mind me staying up with her as long as I didn't talk while she listened to the news and her favorite show, *Johnny Carson*. I never understood what he was talking about, but Mr. Johnny Carson made her laugh so hard. She would be so happy and smiling...a rarity. She would laugh so hard, she'd have to force herself to catch her breath. Sometimes she'd even have to use her inhaler a little extra, which she tried not to do because she was always trying to save her medication as much as possible. But Mr. Carson seemed pretty worth it, and I was glad because I loved watching her. She was hardly ever that happy and full of such joy at the same time.

I remember one morning Mama woke me up and told me it was time to go to school. I had fallen asleep next to her in bed and as she stripped the covers off of me, I whispered that I didn't feel good. And her deep voice quickly snapped, "What did you say?"

I was so tired. "Mami, I feel sick. Maybe I should stay in bed?"

Mama looked at me the way that moms do when they need not say a word and you just know if you don't change quickly, something painful will certainly come your way. She didn't say one word. Didn't need to. Good ol' fear got me out of bed quick! I got up as if a bomb were about to go off underneath me and got dressed fast. I brushed my teeth, combed my hair, ate my tortilla, drank my milk, and sat in the living room waiting to say goodbye to Mama before I left for school. When she walked into the living room, without missing a beat or even turning her head to look at me, she said, "You can stay up as late as you want, the good Lord knows that Johnny Carson is worth it, but you will always go to school just like I have to go to work. That's responsibility. You take responsibility for the choices you make and deal with the consequences. Period. Understood?" I just nodded. And she asked me again, "Didn't hear you. Understood?" And this time, I answered, "Sí, Mami." She then grasped my shoulder as if to help me up, and I knew it would be a long, hard day, but I'd get through it somehow.

Lesson learned. I could make whatever choices I wanted to make, but there would always be costs. And yet, it never stopped me from running into Mama's room most every night to watch—actually, it became kind of a regular thing. I'd fall asleep in my bed, hear her come home, and then I'd run into her bedroom and crawl onto the other side of her bed. I'd only last through part of the monologue, but I'd get to hear Mama laugh and then, I'd just fall asleep next to her, somehow comforted by hearing Ed McMahon's intro, Mr. Carson's voice, *The Tonight Show's* theme music, and my mother's joy in the background.

That's how she did things. She'd teach you the lesson by experience and then, in case you didn't quite grasp it, she'd explain it to you in detail. Afterwards, you were able to make your own decision now that you had the information. Responsibility, consequences, and Johnny Carson.

Now, there were, let's say, "unorthodox" moments too. I only mention it because Mama wasn't perfect. She was close, but only human. And she was always consistent. This moment, although a tough one, was another lesson I'd never forget.

We were in the supermarket and I wanted a piece of candy. Mama was clear. She said no. But, for whatever reason, I went behind her back anyways and grabbed a jawbreaker and plopped it in my mouth.

As soon as I tasted its sour sweetness, I was feeling guilty that I had stolen it. But there was also a part of me that was almost a little proud of myself. I had done something bad without Mama knowing. I had never done anything without Mama knowing, and just as soon as the little proud thought passed in my head, I was choking.

The jawbreaker had gotten lodged in my throat and I couldn't breathe. My mother was a ways ahead of me with the shopping cart and hadn't noticed that I wasn't with her. I tried to cough, but I couldn't get anything out. My eyes were watering and finally Mama turned around. She saw me and seemed to walk calmly towards me. Other people in the store were gathering around concerned and unsure of what to do. One woman was about to kneel down next to me, when my mother said, "Carmen!"

The other women pulled away. Mama looked at me first sternly. The kind of look that said, "That's exactly what you get for stealing and for doing something I told you not to do!" I was little, but I remember that look like it was yesterday. She stared at me with such hardness, such disappointment. Surely it lasted only a split second, but I would never forget that look in her eyes. Twinkle-less.

Mama got me to sit up on the floor and slapped my back hard enough for the jawbreaker to go flying out of my mouth. People around sighed with relief, there were even a few claps, but what came next was more noteworthy.

I had gone against my mother's wishes. I had stolen. That look was all I would ever need. But Mama made sure I understood the lesson. After I was breathing normally, Mama pulled me up by the collar of my shirt. She made me pick up the jawbreaker that had flown across the way and then made me use my own sleeve to clean up the saliva that had gotten on the floor. Oh, and we weren't done. Mama walked me over to the store manager's office so I could apologize for stealing and for making such a scene in the grocery store. To top it all off, Mama didn't finish grocery shopping. She actually started putting back the few items that were in the cart. She was so angry. All she kept saying was that she couldn't believe what I had done. How could I be such a thief? She didn't raise a thief. The manager of the store seemed happy to join in on the scolding of my behavior. He really enjoyed it. Mama was so upset, so disappointed in me… I could hear it in her voice.

I was sent to my room without dinner. And before I went to bed, she came into my room and said to me with no twinkle in her eye at all and no smile on her face, "If you're going to lie, cheat or steal, you better do it right or just don't do it at all. And through my tears I kept trying to say I'm sorry but she wouldn't hear of it. "Sorry's not good enough. I don't know when you decided to become a thief, but that's not the child I know and that's not going to work in this house. It's too complicated to be bad. Now go to bed." She turned off the light and slammed the door shut.

I cried myself to sleep that night.

*　*　*

There were simple things, simple moments that I remember. She would make flour tortillas from scratch on a pretty regular basis. I would watch from a distance as she carefully put all the ingredients together in a glass bowl. She'd then mix everything and begin kneading the dough. It was habitual. The rhythmic motion of forming a ball, and then smoothing out the flat, perfect circles that would be thrown onto the hot oiled frying pan. She'd flip the tortilla over just as quickly as it hit the pan, and then stack them on a red and white checkered towel on top of a dinner plate placed on the warm part of the stove. Usually she'd make them over the weekend and we'd eat them throughout the day. In the early morning, I remember she'd light the match to start the burner on the stove. And for some reason, I always liked the way she'd wave her hand to snuff out the flame of the match. The cast iron pan would get really hot and she'd warm the tortillas in the pan and, after two flips, she'd add butter. I'd watch the butter melt as she'd swirl it all around. I'd start eating it as soon as it was done. Just as my mouth was filled with the buttery goodness, Mama would start her questions about what I'd watched on TV the day before.

I was a latchkey kid. I wore a key around my neck under my clothes. Most days I'd come home to an empty house and go it alone for most of the afternoon and part of the evening till Mama got home. A lot of kids in our neighborhood were latchkey kids. It was normal. She knew the first thing I'd put on was the television. Oh how I loved our TV. Black and white, old, with a broken knob you had to fit just right when it fell off so you could see the other channels. The noise of the TV made the house less scary for me—plus, I loved having the TV on in the background as I was getting ready to go out to rehearsal at the local church. I'd definitely have it on at night before Mama would come home and we'd catch good ol' Johnny Carson together.

Mama wasn't one to repeat herself, so as I waited for the next buttery tortilla to be done, I'd go through the list of what I'd watched the day before. She'd ask for more specifics, "So, what did Archie Bunker do on the show? Did Edith put him in his place?" And I'd answer as best I could, usually with the kid favorite, "I don't know." Even when I wanted to talk about school or rehearsal, she'd go back to what I watched on television, asking me to tell her about every episode of any TV show I watched. And then she would always end with, "Television is not a toy. It's a tool. You need to watch and listen carefully, Carmencita. Remember that." She would then recommended or actually tell me what show I should watch the following day if she wasn't going to be home. Without a doubt— mostly out of fear of doing something wrong and disappointing her—I'd always watch whatever she told me to. That way I'd be ready for any possible questions she might have.

It was her way of keeping tabs on me. I'd learn lessons through some of the shows I watched on television. Throughout the years I talked to my mom about *Sesame Street*, *Gilligan's Island*, *Speed Racer*, *All In The Family*, *Good Times*—she'd even ask me about Johnny Carson's monologue sometimes, just to be funny. We didn't have much time together, but the time we did have was mostly quality time. It prepared me for a time when we would not be together at all.

* * *

She was a good mom. Strict for sure, but good. I saw her as strong and maybe she scared me a little sometimes, but she was also available. She was compassionate and loving without being doting. To love her meant not to disappoint her. Did you see her the same way?

I did ask about you twice. The first time I was about five years old and we lived on Langdon Street in Roxbury. Did you know her when we lived in Boston? Or did you know Mama before, when she lived in New York? Maybe you knew her when she lived in Honduras. But I do remember when I first asked about you, because the image of it all is so embedded in my head. We lived on the second floor and in order to get into the apartment you had to go through two doors. Both doors had windows. Once you did that, you would go up the stairwell that twisted to the right and then you'd be on the landing of our living room area. I liked sitting at the top of that stairwell playing with whatever toys I had in front of me at the time. But this time I was just sitting on the top stair, looking down at the door. Mama stopped and asked me what I was staring at. And so I asked her, "Mami, do I have un Papi?"

In our Spanglish-speaking house you say "Mi Mama" or "Mami" and the same for dad. I would have called you "Mi Papa" or "Papi." Maybe you already knew that. But maybe not because you didn't speak Spanish?

Mama sat down next to me, still wearing her apron from work, with a towel in her hand. She said, "I found you right there, at the bottom of the stairs, in a basket in-between the doors. You were wrapped so tightly. But when I saw you, I knew you were completely all mine. God gave me the best gift by leaving you there." And she winked. And I was so happy! I was completely hers. I was wanted. I didn't know any different. It was my normal.

18

The second time I asked her about you, I was a little older—about ten years old. We lived on Rosemary Street in Jamaica Plain. Mama had been sick and was getting sicker. She had been lying in bed for days. I remember rehearsing in my head what I was going to say and how I would ask. I was so nervous about it. When I asked her, she just looked at me and told me in a very labored and sickly voice, "Carmencita, I promise when you turn sixteen, I will tell you everything about your father."

* * *

The house on Rosemary Street was this old, rickety, three-decker place. It had holes everywhere, and in the cold winter months you could feel the chill streaming in from certain open crevices. Roaches were tenants too, and sometimes you'd see the mice scrambling from one end of the room to the other. They got into the house from the field at the end of the street. There were so many things wrong with this house—stained wallpaper, uneven wood flooring, leaking pipes here and there, holes everywhere where the cold air would seep in. But even though our house was nothing grand to look at, it was somehow still a real beautiful home.

We were pretty poor. But what we did have was valued and taken care of completely. Sundays were always the day we would do chores. Mama was a housekeeper and there was no way other people's homes that she cleaned were ever going to be cleaner than ours. They might have been better homes, richer homes, but they'd never be any cleaner. So every Sunday, we'd get to work.

Mama's prized possession was this old, beautifully carved wooden cabinet that was a record player. When you lifted up the top you would see there was a turntable on the left-hand side, and on the right was a mound of buttons for all the different radio stations. That would be the first thing she would clean. It was heavy. And yet she could move it aside gently like it weighed nothing but a feather. She would dust it, then she'd spray the Raid in the corner wall behind it, and then continue on with Pledge to cover every hand-carved portion of the beautiful flowery design. I'd always cough and she'd open the window to let the air in, but that Raid lemony Pledge combo smell would consume the whole house by the time she was done.

My favorite part: Mama would push back the record player with one gentle shove and then she'd take off her gloves, flip through her records, and stack up several of her favorites. As she cleaned, the house would be filled with the likes of Nat King Cole, Dean Martin, Sammy Davis Jr., Ella Fitzgerald, Louis Armstrong—all the greats. Sometimes you'd hear Elvis, Englebert Humperdinck, maybe even some Neil Diamond, but either way, Mama would sing along and dance as she cleaned. I would watch her move from room to room, dusting along with my own little towel, and loving again how happy she would be.

Music was instant happiness in our house. And I would dance. At some point Mama let me participate in one of the dance programs in the neighborhood. This older woman named Dona Rosita would gather all the little girls in the neighborhood and teach them to dance. We always danced to Puerto Rican-based music, ending always with singing and dancing to one of many "Puerto Rican national anthems" as she would call them. And I would dance my heart out, with such pride about being Puerto Rican. I didn't know it then, but I wasn't Puerto Rican. Even at that young age everyone knew I was a performer at heart. And no matter how poor we were, or whatever badness was going on in my mother's world, even I understood that music equaled happiness. Music and, of course, the great Johnny Carson.

* * *

The best times in our house were around Christmas. We never had any money, but on Christmas Eve and Christmas Day everything was always festive and hopeful.

Mama would always be home early from work on Christmas Eve. She'd walk through the door, take off her long, grey winter coat and, still wearing her apron from working over at the Simon's, she'd get right onto our Christmas feast without skipping a beat. All the classic Christmas songs would be blaring throughout the house; Mama would always be humming or singing along to them under her breath.

There'd be so much more food around, like macaroni and cheese (my favorite), and the very special whole chicken or whole turkey in the oven; sometimes even a pot roast. She was always grateful that her boss or someone at the local school had given us a free chicken or turkey or even a ham, if I remember correctly. I always thought it was kind of nice that they gave out free stuff during the holidays. It was like you worked hard and the world rewarded you with things like chicken and cheese and free milk sometimes. I really did love this time of year!

We also had a beautiful Christmas tree. I loved taking it out of its box and trying to put it together branch by branch. It was a puzzle, but a real-life one. The bigger branch wires fit in the bottom of the thick green pole and the smaller branches went up above. I was too small to stick the prickly branches up on the top. Those were always the coolest because they were so little and yet, still reined on top. That's how I saw it anyways. I hated putting up the lights. The untangling of the wires and making sure the lights were even always seemed to give Mama such trouble. So when it came to that part, I always stepped away. But I always got to put the star on top. That was always my job (with the help of a chair and someone holding me up, of course).

Most everything we had for our Christmas tree was hand-made. So much so, I wasn't really allowed to touch any of the bulbs. There were painted bulbs with pretty pictures depicting everything from the birth of Christ to Frosty the Snowman. Some of the bulbs had decorative textured surfaces, some even had gold flecks and Mama used to say those were the most expensive. Mama would sometimes tell stories of where she got a certain bulb or ornament. She had made a lot of them herself. Or they were given to her by "so and so" and I shouldn't get that close to them just in case. But some of the fancier ones were given to her by someone she worked for or someone saying thanks for something or other. Mama had so many friends, I thought. All of those "special" bulbs were always put at the top of the tree—a little out of my reach anyways.

I was mostly in charge of tinsel throwing. Putting the silvery strings onto the tree that sparkled so pretty. I loved those. I always managed to get more tinsel in my hair than anywhere else. But Christmas would be nothing without staring at Mama's handmade ornaments as they glistened on the tree. They were so fragile. Some were as thin as eggshells and had to be wrapped in tons of toilet paper. Once they were placed on the tree, I would stare at a particular ornament for long periods of time. I was mesmerized by the "sparkly-ness" of it all. Sometimes Mama would yell at me to stop. Reminding me always that if I keep staring, my eyes just might get stuck that way.

One year, I'd gotten it in my head from watching television that I should write a letter to Santa Claus. I mean all the stories we watched—the Claymation animation stuff—always depicted kids writing a letter to Santa and asking him for whatever they wanted. Mama had never encouraged me to write a letter and whenever we did go to the mall to see Santa, she always told me not to ask for anything at all, but to wish him great travels and to give kids who were suffering in Africa what they needed instead. I never said a word to Santa because after all that waiting in line I was so scared to sit on his lap that I couldn't talk even if I tried. Plus, I was such a stutterer and I always preferred to be quiet rather than letting people hear me struggle. I certainly didn't want the great Santa to hear me stutter, so I just stayed quiet instead. Santa always tried, God love him. He'd give up pretty quickly though, and then say I was a sweet kid, pat me on the head, and remind me to keep being good. I always felt bad I never told him to give my gifts to kids in Africa. But goodness knows I ate all the food on my plate regularly and never wasted anything because of them. I always felt good about that.

Now, secretly all I ever wanted was a Barbie. I think that's every little girl's dream—at least back then. And all my friends had Barbies. All the kids in the neighborhood even had the Ken doll, the Townhouse and the fancy pink car that Barbie drove. And so, that's all I ever really wanted: a Barbie.

And a pair of horseback riding boots.

The horseback riding boots were so I could march in the parades and look like everyone else. Mama had put me in the CYO (Catholic Youth Organization) program at the local church so she could work. It was more about free babysitting as far as Mama was concerned, but for me it was about dancing. My passion. I had outgrown the little Puerto Rican dance troupe and we had also moved away from the old neighborhood—what was usually called Jamaica "Spain" (instead of its proper name, Jamaica Plain), as a way to denote its very Latin-esque flavor. We now lived in the "White" part of Jamaica Plain. A whole mile or two down the road but it was another country as far as I was concerned. Everyone seemed mostly Irish. But all of it was still Jamaica Plain, one neighborhood, divided by color. We were the only "Black," "Latino"—basically, dark-skin folk—on the street. But anything I could do to keep performing and dancing, I was game! Later on, it would prove to be one of the best things Mama ever did for me, even if it was accidental.

I got to march in parades whenever they needed someone extra to hold the banner (which started to be all the time). I wore a fancy white pleather skirt, a cowboy vest with that pretty hanging fringe and, if I remember correctly, a red plaid shirt. The problem was that even though the church provided me with the uniform, they didn't have extra boots lying around. So I had to march with pretend boots, which were black tennis sneakers and black plastic leggings that wrapped with elastic under your heel and shoved into your sneakers. From a distance I guess it looked like boots, but everyone knew I didn't have real boots. I knew I had no boots and, well, it was something I had always wanted. I hated being the one without boots, maybe even more than being the only Black kid in the band. I knew Mama could never buy them for me, because they were expensive—they were real leather after all. And we never got anything we didn't need, and hardly ever got anything new. That was the rule. And I'd come to know pretty quickly that I didn't need much at all. So not having boots was a given. Even the kids that did have them, you could tell they were old and worn out. Only the very rich, White kids from the pretty neighborhoods, the good neighborhoods—you know, the ones whose parents had cars and came from places like West Roxbury—had new boots, new everything. I was always so jealous of them.

Even at such a young age, I understood that it wasn't so much the material stuff they had that I was jealous of, but of how sure of themselves it made them. They knew they were better than everyone else. They knew they were better than me. It was in the way they walked, the way they talked, the way they just looked at you. I was jealous. But I kept it all inside with my head held high, just as Mama would have expected me too. But if I was writing a letter to Santa, well, I was going to ask for exactly what I wanted.

So, I started my first letter to Mr. Claus. I was about eight years old at the time. It was short and I just wrote something simple and to the point like: "Dear Mr. Claus, this is Carmen. I've been a real good girl—Mama even said so. I know I should give my gifts to kids in Africa, but I was wondering if just this year you could please send me one Barbie doll and a pair of black leather horseback riding boots so I can march in the parade and look like everybody else. I promise to take care of my boots and I promise to take care of my Barbie. Thank you very much, Carmen. PS, I love you." I put it in an envelope and addressed it to "Mr. Santa Claus, The North Pole," and when I walked to school the next day, I put my letter in the mailbox all by myself. It was the first letter I'd ever mailed.

It was Christmas Eve and Mama had cooked as she always did. Other family and friends had stopped by and the house was full of smells, people, and good cheer. I couldn't wait to get to bed. As soon as I could, I excused myself and said goodnight. Mama reminded me to check that she'd put the cookies and milk in the right place for Santa before I went to bed. I ran into the living room to double-check everything and, after a few adjustments, I stepped back into the kitchen briefly, said goodnight again to everyone, and went right off to bed.

That night was magical. I'm positive I heard the footsteps of reindeer on the rooftop for sure. Santa most definitely landed on the house, and jingling bells and the clitter-clatter of hoofs were absolutely there that Christmas Eve. I heard it clearly and, because I didn't want to mess anything up by being awake, I huddled under the covers even more, kept my eyes shut, and didn't dare move a muscle.

I must have fallen asleep because I remember waking and sitting straight up in my bed, letting the covers fall off my shoulders, leaving me cold and yet completely excited! It was always chilly in our house that time of year. Mama rarely put on the heat at night, so you could always see your breath in the morning. I pulled on my sweater, fixed my socks, threw on my slippers, wrapped my scarf around my neck, and put on my mittens. I went out into the living room and saw that Santa had drunk just a tiny bit of the milk and only left one cookie on the plate. I knew he liked chocolate chip cookies, just like me. As I looked around the room I didn't see any gifts under the tree, and for a moment my heart sank. Then I realized we didn't have a chimney, so of course the presents wouldn't be under the tree! They must be outside on the porch. The bag full of presents must've been too heavy! We really should get a chimney someday, I thought to myself.

I quickly went down the stairs, skipping two at a time, and tried to open the lock as best I could. Finally I took off my mittens to fling open the latch, and opened the door. And there it was: the box! A huge box with a label and other markings on its side. Obviously Santa had been rushing and had accidentally left the box upside down, so it was possible some of the presents had tipped over. I hoped they hadn't broken. I knew for sure that my Barbie and my horseback riding boots would be just fine.

I heard the sound of the electric heater cranking so I knew Mama was awake. She saw me struggling to put the box right-side up. She smiled from the top of the stairs and motioned for me to wait—she'd be right down to help me. Eventually we got the box up into the living room and I waited patiently as I watched the tape being peeled off. Mama then gave the okay to go at it. I went to the box that was larger than me and started eagerly pulling out the unwrapped items. A board game, white tube socks, a blue ski hat, ladies stockings, cans of Campbell's tomato soup, Campbell's chicken soup, cans of SpaghettiOs, cans of beans and corn, a box of crayons, colored paper (like the kind you get in school), coloring books, Legos, a Chinese checkers game, a yo-yo, a baseball mitt, and a big, huge, ugly doll that was half the size of me and whose legs didn't bend at the knees.

No Barbie. No boots.

I stared at the opened empty box as tears welled up in my eyes. My mom was looking at the stockings and trying to figure out if she would be able to wear them and if they didn't fit who she could give them to. And when she looked up, I was staring at the emptied box. She saw my eyes well up. She could tell how sad I was. She looked at the big, ugly doll and asked me if I liked it. She told me that when she talked to Santa and told him how beautiful a child I was and that I had been so good all year, that she couldn't help but ask him to please bring me a very special doll. "This exact one," she said, almost too excitedly. She mentioned that even though kids in Africa needed it more than we did, that I deserved a very special doll. And so she asked Santa to send this very special one to me.

But that's how I knew—there was no Santa Claus. The Salvation Army wasn't Santa's local office after all.

Seeing my mother's face, I immediately tried to smile. I told her in my best voice that I loved it, that I was so happy Santa brought me any gift at all. My chest hurt. I was ready to bawl-out cry. She knew. And even though I pretended to be okay, I hated the non-bending-at-the-knee ugly doll. I hated it. I wasn't fooling anyone.

I dealt with Christmas the way I always did amongst my neighborhood friends—like it didn't matter. They would all show off their new pretty clothes, the latest toys; some even had new gold jewelry, like bracelets and necklaces. I would simply be happy for them and pretend I'd gotten important stuff I asked for, things like dancing shoes, expensive dancing tights, leg warmers—everything you needed to be a dancer and things I could never just bring out on the streets. I mean, that would be ridiculous, right? Of course it was a lie, but they believed it because I was so…believable. They didn't participate in anything but school stuff with me anyways, so it's not like they'd find

27

out. And I never was one to ask for anything at all, certainly never asking Santa for things like toys. Somehow my lies, or my improvisations, always worked out. They worked out so well that I even started to believe them.

One early Saturday morning Mama came to me as I fussed with the TV antenna. I thought she might yell at me for touching it at all, but instead she told me to get dressed, that we had to go run some errands. My face must have shown signs of disappointment—I was going to miss some important show like *Super Friends*, *Gilligan's Island* or *The Banana Splits* or something—because Mama then said to me in a very stern voice, "Don't even start, just get dressed and hurry up. Don't make me ask you again."

And so I got dressed. And we left.

It had snowed quite a bit and it was a feat just to walk up the street to the corner bus stop, but we made it just in time to catch the bus. I watched my mother sitting next to me, wearing her glasses, reading a map and some directions, and I made the mistake of asking her where we were going. Without moving a muscle, she said quietly, almost like a ventriloquist, "Behave yourself. You'll know when we get there."

Behave yourself meant you don't talk on the bus, you don't fidget in your seat. You're quiet and do not cause any problems whatsoever. Mama was very strict on rules. And I was really good at following them. Mama used to say that just because we were poor didn't mean we had to behave like poor folk. So proper etiquette was key. Not that my Mama made me be fancy or anything like that, but she always thought it best, when in doubt, to be quiet and humble. Always be clean. Wear the best you can. Stand tall, chin up, and you could never go wrong if you kept your mouth shut (especially around rich folk, which in our neighborhood really meant White folk).

We got off the trolley and then boarded two more connecting buses. I was starting to get antsy and annoyed, but Mama would just look at me out the corner of her eye

28

and I'd straighten up and get right back on track. Fearing I'd get in trouble if I let out one more sigh, I easily found interest in whatever was outside the window passing us by.

Finally we got off the bus. We walked in the snow for what seemed to be forever. My legs were hurting and my toes were pretty cold. I held Mama's hand tightly, looking at all the fancy houses across the way. Pretty Christmas decorations hung from the windows and huge statues of reindeer and Santas sat in most of the front lawns. Every house was different, but beautiful and magical nonetheless. Someone had made a real Frosty the Snowman and used a real carrot for the nose. I wondered if the eyes and mouth were food too. But I couldn't see that far. What a waste of good food, I thought. But oh how very cool!

We kept walking till eventually we made it to this beautiful little village shopping center. It looked like something you'd see on television in one of those afterschool specials. The sidewalks were plowed, people were walking joyously in the streets, and the store windows were picture-perfect "Christmassy." There were trees lining the street, they were covered with snow and had long, pretty icicles hanging from the bare branches. I couldn't believe Mama had brought me with her to such a pretty place, and I kept thinking how glad I was I had put on my best sweater, because this was definitely a special place to be. I wondered, as we walked along, if Mama was going to get a new job here or something. If she worked here, in one of these big houses, she'd make a lot of money, I thought to myself.

We walked and walked and Mama kept stopping along the way to look at her map and then she'd look up at the store signs and the street signs. As always, I kept silent. My hand was tightly in hers as I watched all the pretty people walking on by. I just kept taking in all the wonderful sights. I wish I lived here, I thought. And I wish we drove that car. I wish that was me, playing on the snow mound with my fancy parka with fur around the hood. I wish we had a dog that I could walk on a long leash… Mama tugged me as she started to move onward and knocked me out of my wishful fantasy. We turned the corner and I saw it—the place Mama was looking for.

As we walked up closer, I could see a rare smile on my Mama's face. She looked at me out the corner of her eye again, but this time she turned her head and gave me a big smile. Tears had welled up in my eyes and I swear, like a picture-perfect moment, one tear streamed down one side of my cheek. She stopped, turned to me, and knelt for a moment in the snow. She said quietly, "Carmencita, we're going in that store for one thing and only one thing. And I can only get it for you if it's still on sale, okay? So behave yourself and don't ask for anything else. You can look, but do not touch anything."

I nodded quickly and happily. She let go of my hand and I walked really fast, almost ran, but remembered to keep with proper etiquette. I tried with all my might to open the door. Mama came up from behind me and helped push the door open, and the little jingling bells made that "chime-y" noise to let the store owner know that someone was here.

And there they were.

Right in front of me, it looked like hundreds of them lined up perfectly along the whole side of the store— horseback riding boots. I stared at them for the longest time. I didn't touch, didn't even go that close to them. I looked at them from a distance. Just like I looked at Mama's beautiful ornaments on our Christmas tree that I was never allowed to touch. In the center of the wall there were cowboy boots of all designs. Some were plain, but most had beautiful stitching on them, and silver tips, and that weird wheely thing on the back that only real cowboys ever really needed. I was overwhelmed and staring at everything in the store. Belts and silvery stuff everywhere. All sorts of boots, hats and vests. And I thought, real cowboys must certainly shop here. You know, when they come to Boston anyways.

Mama had gone to talk to the salesperson and even though I couldn't hear what was going on, I could tell he wasn't being very nice to her at all. That was normal. I mean, we weren't in our neighborhood after all and, well, that's just the way things were back then.

The mean man came over to me and told me to sit and take off my boots. He was gruff and never once even looked me in the eye. I struggled to take off my boots myself. I had on two pairs of socks and stockings, so my boots were on really tight. Mama finally came over and helped me. When my boots came off, you could see the holes in my socks. To my embarrassment, they were also a little wet. Mama was embarrassed too. But they were the socks I was supposed to wear with these boots in the snow because usually I'd wear these boots and never dream of taking them off unless I was in the house. Now I wished I had put on my school socks instead, but Mama would have killed me for sure if I had done that. I don't know, maybe not.

Anyway the mean salesman pushed my foot in the metal thing to check my size. He told me to take off the socks and my mom, in a very humble voice, told him no, that we wanted them to fit a size bigger so I could wear them longer. He looked at her with such a cruel face and said, "These aren't boots for the snow. These are leather. You can't wear them in the snow. They're not for playing outside." He talked to her like she was stupid. Mama, finding her composure, looked him straight in the eye and without missing a beat said, "Thank you so much. But she won't be wearing them in the snow." And he walked away, mumbling something under his breath, to fetch the boots.

Mama stood there, looking at me. I sat quietly and looked back at her. I thought she might have been mad at me about the holes in my socks or disturbed that this man talked to her like she wasn't smart. But she winked at me and I smiled even more. The man returned with a huge box and took out the most beautiful black horseback riding boots I'd ever seen. He helped me put them on and I walked around the store for a bit. Obviously, they were a little big, but perfect nonetheless. The backs of the boots were too long and pierced the back of my knees, and when I told Mama she mentioned it to the nasty clerk. He said sternly, "Well, of course you'll have to get them cut, but that'll cost you. It'll cost you quite a bit. We don't do that for free. And you know these aren't on sale. No sirree. You'll have to pay full price."

My face went blank. Mama had told me earlier if they weren't on sale, we couldn't buy them. And the man started pulling off the boots from my feet, sure that Mama couldn't buy them anyways. He mumbled something again under his breath and though I strained to hear him I couldn't really make it out. But I'm sure the phrase "Black" or "nigger" and "no good for nothing" and something else came out of his mouth. That was normal with White folk like that, it always was.

I watched his hands as he packed up the boots in the big white box, knowing I'd never see them again. I was so sad, but I kept it all inside. I was trying to anyways. And then, out of nowhere, Mama, who now seemed a few inches taller, stepped in front of the despicable clerk and pulled from her purse more money than I'd ever seen. With confidence, and a bit more loudly than I'd ever heard Mama speak to anyone, let alone a White man, she counted out every cent. Ten, twenty, thirty dollars…and so on and so on. Then she politely said, "I think that's correct. You should double-check it to make sure. I've included a little extra for a tip. Please put those in a bag for us, with handles if you have one, and we'll be on our way. I certainly do appreciate your kindness and help today."

It was a frozen moment in time. I'll never forget it. The man's face seemed floored that Mama could speak English properly or something. Or that she had enough money and then some to pay for the boots. I have no idea. But she went from struggling, old, meek housekeeper to an elegant, fierce, business-matter-of-fact woman in a matter of seconds, and the clerk realized that the woman he was speaking to was not going to play this game with him. And she was offering him a tip, treating him with dignity and respect regardless of his bad behavior. I was so proud.

He gathered the boots and the box and quietly said, "Yes, ma'am. Thank you ma'am." And before I knew it, I had the bag and box in my hand. When we left the store, the pathetic clerk even wished us well and told us to come back again soon. My mom didn't even look his way or say goodbye herself. I knew we'd never find ourselves in that store ever again.

When we finally got on the first bus back towards our neighborhood, my mom's demeanor relaxed and went back to normal. It was late and there weren't many people on the bus at all. I had a smile on my face and didn't fidget or sigh or anything. I had been dreaming about how everyone was going to see me in my new boots. For the first time I'd have something brand new. And they were all mine!

But as I looked at my mom, I saw that she was crying. I'd never seen her cry. She looked over at me and attempted a smile but I could tell she was thinking a million things. She hugged me as I embraced the shopping bag with all my might. She sniffled and then caressed my hair as the bus went along. She spoke in Spanish and quietly so no one else would hear, "I used extra money that I was supposed to use to pay for the heat, Carmencita, so you could have those boots. They were supposed to be on sale, but...well, it doesn't matter, you deserve them." She wiped her nose with her Kleenex and then hastily added, "And Santa would have brought them to you himself but he just couldn't this year. He's very busy, you know. It's gonna be cold in the house all the time now for a little while, but you have your boots and I expect you'll take good care of them, okay?" And I replied, "Yes, Mami. I promise."

I never figured out how Mama knew I wanted those boots. And I never did get a Barbie doll. But I wore those boots for as long as I could remember. They cut through the back of my knees and broke the skin the first parade I marched in. Blood dripped into the back of my boots the whole time, but I didn't care. I marched so proudly anyways. When the parade ended, one of the fathers of one of the other little girls helped clean up the blood on my legs and bandaged me up real good. He took my boots, cleaned them, and told me he'd get them cut for me. And he did. I wore those boots every time I could—till they had holes in them. And then, we just got them resoled.

That's one of my favorite childhood memories. I learned so much that day. It was the year I learned there was no Santa. Or actually, the year I learned who Santa really was.

Sadly, Mama would never see me perform. She never watched me in a parade or ever came to any of my performances or even rehearsals. I doubt she ever even noticed me practicing outside on the street in the early morning, when she'd call me in through the window to get ready for school, or at night for dinner. The boots would be the only memory I have of Mama acknowledging my performing life. And although some would see that as really sad, I don't. The boots were validation. The boots were love.

* * *

Christmastime. I always thought about you even more that time of year. The perfect family was always two parents, a dog, and a white picket fence. The holidays were hard.

When people treated Mama like she was dirt, I imagined what you might've done if you were there. Of course, it was always superhero-like. You'd come, beat someone up, and save the day. You'd pick me up over your shoulder and I'd laugh into your arms. But just as soon as I'd have the thought, it'd vanish.

A part of me hoped you kept in touch with Mama even if you never talked to me. But another part of me knew better. If you had been in touch, the days Mama was so sick, you would have helped her, you would have been there for her. Anyone would have. No decent person would have watched someone suffer so much. It just isn't possible.

* * *

If Mama wasn't working, she was sick. She would tell me easily and simply it was asthma, but asthma might as well have been cancer. She was taking so many prescription drugs, using an inhaler, and could never sleep too well, even with the loud humidifier on in her room. Mama always looked hurting to me. She had lost that happy gleam in her eyes, her twinkle was barely there. She was still powerful and could scare me just by her look, but beneath the disciplined strong woman was an ever-growing pain that was slowly eating away at her.

I did what I could to stay out of her way. She had already died twice in the hospital—that's what I called it, anyway. Back then if you weren't at least twelve years old, they wouldn't let you go in to see someone who was in the hospital unless they were being given last rights. Twice, not fully understanding where my mother was going, I was invited into the room while the priest was there to give her last rights. My mother would motion to me, through the tubes in her nose and mouth and needles stuck in her arms, that she loved me. And I'd smile back and say I loved her too. And then I'd be whisked out of the room and sat in the waiting room only to go home a few hours later. Then, days later, Mama would be back home making tortillas and talking to me about school. I'd say I was confused, but I didn't know what dying really meant. To me, it meant a few days without Mama because she was in the hospital, but she'd be home later. Because that's exactly what would happen.

It was the summer of 1979. Mama had allowed me, more than once, to stay at some of the other girls' houses when I was doing back-to-back competitions with the local CYO group. I had gotten really good and was addicted to rehearsals and performing. Mrs. Connelly offered to let me stay with her for two weeks, since it was the end of the summer and we'd been rehearsing daily and driving to competitions far away. Mrs. Connelly's two kids were also in the same program so it was perfect. Mama let me go without hesitation. I remember running out of the house with my bag of clothes, screaming as I jumped down the stairs, "Thank you, Mami. Thank you, thank you! See you in two weeks!" I never heard her say anything back.

Two weeks later, August 28, after our successful tours and competition, Mrs. Connelly drove me back home. When we got to my street, there were cop cars everywhere, an ambulance careening past us, and all the neighbors were outside. As we pulled up as near to my house as possible, I could see the door was open, a cop was standing in the doorway, and there seemed to be so many people inside. I jumped out the back of the station wagon. Mrs. Connelly tried to call me back to the car as I ran to my house to see what was going on.

I walked into the doorway to see people milling around along the stairwell. People were talking, but under their breath. No one really noticed me, but I could hear Mrs. Connelly trying to find out what was happening.

Eventually, I found my way to my room and I shut the door. I didn't understand what was happening, but I didn't like all the people in the house. I heard a knock on the door. Mrs. Connelly opened it and stepped in. "Are you okay, Carmen? Do you want to stay here or come back with us? You're always welcome to come home with us."

I didn't understand why she was asking me such a thing. But I shook my head no and told her I was fine and that I was just going to go to bed. And she looked at me so kindly and then simply, very quietly, shut the door.

When the noise subsided a bit and I heard people leaving, I ventured outside to look for Mama. There were still people in the house, mostly people I knew from the neighborhood, but some I didn't. Some were wailing, crying, others mostly mumbling under their breath. I went to my mother's room, and as I turned into the doorway, I saw a man put my mother's Bible on her bed. He turned, and as he walked passed me, he patted me on the head and continued on.

I was eleven and a half years old. Standing in my mother's doorway. Staring, gazing, at the Bible on her bed. No one told me she died. It wasn't that they forgot; it was that everyone thought someone else had told me, I guess. I was a strong kid, a quiet kid, and by all accounts, a really good kid. But that mistake—no one telling me, no one comforting me, no one explaining it at all to me—that moment would change me forever.

I was alone. And I knew it.

* * *

I didn't think of you at all then. You weren't even a passing thought. Even though I was old enough and I should have understood, I didn't. I thought somehow I would see her again if I just waited. I thought we'd be eating tortillas with melted butter and talking about Johnny Carson and All In The Family. Moments kept playing in a loop in my head— sun-kissed cinnamon skin, responsibilities, consequences, don't be conceited, television is not a toy, etiquette, manners, dignity, pride, her smile, her belly-aching laugh—all of it so I wouldn't forget. And with my hand, I'd hold my chest and slow my breathing. I'd promise myself never to be afraid. That I just had to listen closely and she'd be right here.

The middle of it all...

Oma

Chaos. I was standing in the middle of a large room watching a bunch of out of control adults scrambling around me. Mama was gone. People were screaming, crying, yelling, arguing, fighting. Sorrow and pain all around. I couldn't stop taking it all in. My whole body just kept trying to absorb it all. No one talked to me. No one even looked at me. It was like I wasn't even there.

Other people, "relatives," were now staying in the house. I think it's a very Latino thing, but for years I grew up thinking everyone who lived in the neighborhood was related to me in some way, shape, or form. I was taught at a young age that anyone who was an elder or even just some years older than me was an aunt or an uncle. It's a sign of respect. When Mama died, I had more "family" than I'd ever seen in my entire life. Tia "this" or Tio "that." Translation: Aunt "this" or Uncle "that." I didn't talk to any of them. Most of them were liars. "Bonchichetta," Mama used to say. Translation: Gossipers. These were the types of people that, when it suited them, were your best friend, but when there was nothing in it for them, nothing to gain, they were nowhere to be found. Sad. None of them were really all that interested in me anyway. It was all a show. Truth is, most days no one ever really noticed I was even in the room.

As far as I was concerned, my world was only about me and Mama, school, and dancing. These were just neighborhood folk—the same "relatives" who couldn't loan her money when she needed to buy medicine, and wouldn't babysit me when she had to work or had an emergency. Mama always helped people no matter what.

And I remember seeing Mama upset sometimes because she'd gone out of her way to help someone and they didn't return the favor. Even still, Mama helped people. Even those who often let her down. It was the right thing to do. Etiquette. And now these "relatives" were staying in Mama's house, in Mama's room, going through Mama's things. It bothered me but I couldn't think of anything to do about it.

They'd always speak in Spanish, sometimes too fast but, for the most part, I could understand. They were discussing my mother's belongings—what they could sell or what they would keep. They talked about my mother's stuff as if she'd been rich or something. And then they'd talk badly about her when they didn't like some cheap piece of clothing or costume jewelry. They either didn't think I knew Spanish or thought I wasn't listening. But I was paying so much attention, and I knew exactly what they were saying. And I was hating all of them more with every day that passed on by.

And then "Tia" Cecelia started listening to my mother's records. I was sitting in my room feeling my heart race when I heard the first notes of Frank Sinatra. How dare anyone touch my mother's stuff, especially her beautiful wooden record player! And Tia Cecelia was singing loudly with her Spanish accent and dancing all around the living room. I had walked out of my room and stood in the hallway watching her. She caught me when she finished a twirl around the living room chair. She stared at me for a moment and then ordered me to go back to my room "where I belonged." I stormed back to my room and slammed the door. A few moments later, she threw the door open and told me that I was a horrible, ungrateful child and that I was probably the reason why my poor mother dropped dead. She yelled it all in Spanish. Then she pretended to translate it for me. She said, "Your mother would not be happy with the way you sneak around and watch people. You should not be so sneaky.

Now stay in this room until I tell you otherwise." Her translations were always different than what she actually said, but I didn't see any reason to correct her. She wouldn't have listened anyway.

I wasn't so confused about things. I knew inside what most people really thought of me. And if I had ever been a little confused, these ladies sitting at my mother's kitchen table were making it quite clear: "Emma always thought that little runt was better than all the other kids, well she's not." It was a common theme and always in Spanish as if I was clueless. In their view, I was a problem child. Like a little devil, and not in a good way. I was quiet and kept to myself. They didn't like that at all. I participated in very "American" things, which meant very "White" things, and, on top of it all, I didn't talk much—mostly because I stuttered. They didn't get that. I never spoke too much. Not in front of them. To them I was a loner. I'd cry in my pillow most nights. All I wanted was Mi Mama back. I kept hoping Mama would just return. That this was just a bad dream. But with every day that passed, I knew this was my new reality. Mama would never come back.

Tia Cecelia didn't like me at all. Behind my back she would call me names in Spanish that roughly translated to an "ungrateful child" and her regular favorite: "the devil." She would say it to my face with that painted-red-lipstick smile. She really thought I didn't know Spanish. And who was I to tell her differently? She was a typical Latino lady in her fifties trying to look twenty, wearing her black-blue-dyed hair in a tight bun, with pale, white, powdery skin, and always too much red lipstick. She had those ultralong nails with the same red color to match. I wouldn't have called her my mother's friend if a gun was at my temple, but there she was, evil and mean. Going through her deceased, supposed "best friend's" things and sorting through what she'd keep, what she could sell, and what she'd throw out. My mother hadn't been gone a week yet.

Mama's funeral was amazing… mostly in a bad way. It was held at Blessed Sacrament, the school I went to and the church was filled to maximum capacity with people filling in the side aisles—standing room only. I sat in front, and, as I knelt on the bench in the first pew, I was still stunned by all that had happened in the last week. I could hear the milling of people coming into the church behind me. The noise was so loud, though everyone seemed to be trying to whisper and at the same time trying to be quiet. But the high ceilings echoed everything. People were talking and tearing up and crying—and I turned around and noticed how large the crowd really was. I couldn't believe it. All these people. All these people knew my mother, loved my mother or thought so highly of her! This wasn't a small church; this was a pretty big church, and I don't think I'd ever seen it filled. At first I couldn't believe my eyes and I was proud at how amazing my mother truly was to everyone…

And then I saw Tia Cecelia.

She walked down the aisle with two men trying to hold her up on either side. She appeared so physically grief stricken. When she got to my aisle, the front pew, she looked at me to move over and I did so quickly. And then, out of nowhere, she took out these weird small dolls and started chanting some strange, old-world voodoo type of thing. I was shocked. She was making a scene. My mother would have cringed at such a display. My mother was simple and, although poor, she was classy, even conservative. She would have never been okay with this. In a Catholic church no less! And now people were whispering. She kept looking at me out of the corner of her eye—and you would think I'd have been scared, but I knew she was just working the crowd. Crying and singing all that old-country religion crap wasn't going to fool me, and I lost it. I started screaming at her and told her to get out. She tried to grab me and make me sit down. Instead, I jumped over the small pew wall. I turned to the crowd and started yelling at all of them, "Why are you all here now? Where were you when Mami needed you? How could you all be such hypocrites? All of you get out! Get out!"

Father Walsh rushed over to calm me down. My heart was racing. My eyes filled with tears. And now I was embarrassed. But I knew, deep down, I was right. Mama might have been mad at me, disappointed even, but maybe slightly proud of me nonetheless. Someone needed to say something. Sister Corina and Sister Francesca, both teachers I respected in the school, calmed me down and walked me out of the church. They brought me over to the convent. In all the years I'd gone to school there, I'd never known anyone to have gone into the convent that wasn't a nun. But I sat there, with both of them, as they talked to me about something or other. I didn't say a word. I sat on an old maroon velvety couch, staring at the wooden floor for what seemed to be hours. I missed the funeral. And the burial. I never got to see where Mama was buried.

There were others in the neighborhood, besides Tia Cecelia, trying to lay claim to my mother's belongings. As little as my Mama owned, it seemed to be a gold mine in our neighborhood. Lots of people attempted to befriend me and to be my guardian at one point or another, but Tia Cecelia would eventually win out over all of them. And she was the worst. She'd pretend to care for me and love me. "As if she were my own daughter," she'd say to the judge hearing the case as to who would be my legal guardian. And yet, most days, Tia Cecelia never even knew where I was. In court her English would magically become broken and she could barely understand what the big, important judge was saying. It was all an act. An act so she could hopefully lay claim to Mama's house and Mama's belongings. Whoever was my guardian would inevitably be the owner of a rundown, roach-infested, three-decker house in Jamaica Plain. In our neighborhood, that was equal to being rich.

I was dragged to court more times than I care to recall. And each time I hoped the court would rule against Tia Cecelia but to no avail. I always wished the judge would ask me what I wanted, but he never asked me anything at all. I remember being so frightened by it all. When I look back on it, I wish I had screamed as loudly as I did in the church that day about Tia Cecelia, about my mother, but I never did. Tia Cecelia, with the bright red lipstick, would be my guardian at least until the next court date. And that's when things got real bad.

It wasn't that Tia Cecelia was a bad person—at least that's what I wanted to believe. She just wanted a better life. And this was her opportunity. Unfortunately, I was in the way. Maybe I was just a nuisance. She definitely didn't have any kids, and she didn't seem to like me at all, so clearly this wasn't going to be easy for anyone. Plus, unbeknownst to me, I had a reputation in the neighborhood. I was a "snob." I was "La Americana." And my mother clearly thought I was better than all the other kids; that's why she let me hang around the White kids in West Roxbury or those rich Black people in Roxbury. Somehow I wasn't Latina enough. I would hear some of the older adults talk about me as if I'd done something wrong, that me and my mother were in denial or something. The amount of hatred towards me was…sad. Even I knew—and I was just a kid! I didn't understand it. To my face, they'd say one thing. Some would talk extra nice to me, but I knew it was a lie. In Spanish (not even behind my back), they'd say something else. And it always made me feel so horrible, so hurt. I didn't know what I had done. But I never said a word. My saving grace was that I still always had dancing. Winter Guard. School. People there liked me a lot. Loved me just for being me, in fact.

What I started to realize about my new life on Rosemary Street, in my Mama's house, was that as long as I wasn't physically around, in Tia Cecelia's eyesight, things were fine. But if I made myself known in any way, shape, or form, then we'd have a problem. Or, I should say, I'd have a problem. Normally, it would just consist of her screaming at me—for, say, watching TV in my mother's room. It was the only room with a TV so I would come home after school and watch my shows just like I always did. She would come into the room and ask me what I was doing in "her" room. I could never understand why she was there during the day. Didn't she work like Mama used to? It was so uncomfortable to be in Mama's room. In my own house. And Tia Cecelia wouldn't waste a second; she'd send me to my room and tell me that things were going to change because she was now in charge. No more TV for me. My daily routine, disrupted.

I adjusted. I just tried my best to.

I'd disappear. Do the "avoid" thing. I'd stay out later after school. The first time I wondered if I'd get in trouble when I walked in the door so late, but Tia Cecelia would be at the table with some neighborhood friends or some "uncles" talking and smoking and drinking and they wouldn't even notice that I'd come in the door. Staying out after school, hanging on the street, was not a bad thing for me after all. It was better than coming home and having to hide in my room forever, till rehearsal or until the next day for school.

And that's how it went for a while. I was sad. Maybe even miserable. But when I left my house I could forget about it all and I could be me, the old me, the normal me. Everyone at rehearsal was super nice to me and my teachers and classmates were so kind. But everyone thought I was just sad because Mama died. I guess that makes sense. But it was also because I had no one to talk to. No one person really cared about me or for me. I'd go to rehearsal and be the star I always was—but my dancing was slipping too. I wasn't allowed to rehearse in the mornings anymore and I wasn't sleeping very well or eating regularly. I was always scared about getting yelled at when I got home. I tried to be perfect at rehearsal, invisible at home. I always tried to be good. But I always messed up somehow as far as Tia Cecelia was concerned.

And then one day it came to blows.

I came home and no one was around so I grabbed myself a bowl of cereal and sat at the kitchen table and listened to the radio. I remember I was eating Fruit Loops. I had two bowls. When I was done, I put the milk back in the fridge, the cereal back on the shelf, and put my bowl and spoon in the sink. I left a little later for rehearsal and returned later that evening.

When I walked in the front door, on the stairwell was the cereal bowl. On the next stair step was a spoon. The bowl was halfway filled with water and milk. I was unsure what it was doing there so I walked around it thinking it was none of my business. When I got to the landing, there was Tia Cecelia. She was angry. She started yelling at me about leaving dishes in the sink and that she wasn't my maid and a whole bunch of other stuff. She yelled at me to pick up the bowl and the spoon and told me that if I ever left another dish in the sink she would leave them on the stairwell for me to clean up as soon as I got home. And that was that.

I picked up the bowl and the spoon and headed on into the kitchen. She followed me, still screaming about something or other and, although I was so angry, I was doing my best to keep it all inside. I threw the bowl and the spoon into the sink and the bowl shattered into many pieces. I started to apologize and went to grab a paper bag to pick up the broken bits just like Mama used to do, but Tia Cecelia grabbed me by the hair and threw me into the corner. She was screaming at me in Spanish and talking so fast I could barely understand her. I landed on the floor near the stove. I put my hands up to protect myself, and she must've thought I was going to fight back, because she then grabbed both my hands and threw me to the other side of the kitchen. My whole body slammed into the back doorway. My head took the brunt of it, and it took me a second to come to. I slowly got myself up, and grabbed the doorknob, and stumbled down the back stairs. She followed me, screaming and yelling, and the neighbors were all out now and could hear everything. She had lost her mind. I ran across two neighbors' backyards and finally escaped her by sneaking up a tiny alleyway. Ms. Oma, a little old German lady who always sat in her wheelchair on her porch and never said a word to anyone, motioned to me to step into her house. I didn't know what to do, but I knew Mama used to bring her soup sometimes when she made too much, so I went inside and sat quietly on the floor of her living room.

After a little while, the commotion outside on the street died down. Tia Cecelia seemed to have gone back inside with some of her friends and the immediate threat was over. I kept thinking about what was going to happen when I eventually went home. Mama had never hit me before. She never threw me against a wall. I could feel a huge bump on my head right above my eye where I had hit the door. I kept touching it and wondering what it looked like. I was scared, but I knew for the moment, as I sat here, I was safe.

Ms. Oma wheeled her chair into the house and went past the living room only to return shortly afterwards. She still didn't say a word. She just looked at me and motioned with her hands to come to her. I knelt by her wheelchair, grateful to her for letting me hide in her home. On her lap she had an envelope. She took out some money in different bills and handed them to me. It was a bunch of singles and fives and some tens. I counted it: $107. She looked at me and put her old, shaky hand onto my cheek and said, "You run. You run now." And I looked into her eyes and I lost it. I cried so hard. I couldn't control myself. Ms. Oma just looked at me. She let me cry for a long time.

My world had changed. I knew I had to run too.

That was the last night I stayed on Rosemary Street.

Jarrod

There's no doubt being part of the dance group in the neighborhood started out as just a convenient babysitting situation for my mom. I'd be at the neighbors or, later, I'd be at the church rehearsing, and she'd know I was safe. But after my mother died, dancing and performing became even more of an obsession for me. It would become an addiction. A good addiction, in fact.

One of my favorite memories of living in our old house on Rosemary Street was when I was just a little girl, maybe seven or eight years old. I'd wake up at five o'clock in the morning and put on my old shoes, using electrical tape around the soles and tops to make them fit tighter and grab a little easier on the cardboard box I'd use as my dance floor. I would go out in front of the house underneath the street lamplight and begin my own personal rehearsal. I'd stare into the cars that were lined up before me, and the shadows would mold into this huge crowd of people waiting to watch me perform. I'd dance my heart out. The lamplight would flicker and the sun would just be coming up to give that beautiful golden glow and my performance would be done. But as I'd go to leave, there'd be a clamoring by the shadows. "Just one more time!" I swear I'd hear the crowd yell out. And so, of course, as to not let my shadowy fans down, I'd perform an encore.

Joaquin, an older neighborhood boy, would always come by on his paper route riding his black Huffy bike and he'd wave to me—signaling that it was time to get back in the house and get ready for school. This routine continued even after Mama died. Now though, I was beginning to find cracks in my pretending she wasn't actually dead, but just always at work. I was missing the tiniest of things. Her quick glance at me to make sure I looked decent for school, the morning lectures on TV watching while eating breakfast, tortillas and melted butter—those all disappeared. I missed how she'd run out to get to work. And now, when I'd put my keychain over my head and under my blouse, nothing seemed to matter all that much. I'd grab my book bag and walk to the bus stop to get to school.

The thing that excited me most was dancing and band practice. I'd become quite the performer, and loved being in the rifle section of the Winter Guard. I was so good. All those years as a little girl participating in the local neighborhood dance group had paid off. I had gone from Dona Rosita's little Puerto Rican dancing group and worked my way into the White folks' local marching band at the church. I marched in local parades and danced with the team at local events put on in our neighborhood. At some point the marching band let me officially be part of the Winter Guard—that's the part of the band that interprets the music through the use of flags, rifles, sabers, and, more importantly to me, dancing. I had become a fan of using the rifle, along with my dancing "expertise" at the young age of eight, to express myself. And so those mornings out in front of the house now became a combination of dancing and amazing spinning rifle work for my shadowy fans. And in the process, I became good. I had learned to do cool things that only certain older teenagers were doing, like flips and somersaults. I had become a little star in my neighborhood—this "other" part of the neighborhood, not just because people were impressed with how I could spin a rifle and dance my butt off, but also because I was so committed and dedicated. Other parents in the neighborhood would make note of it as they reprimanded their own kids or tried to use my obsession, maybe dedication, as encouragement. Either way, it just added to the natural high I got from performing. I loved it.

I would hear other grownups talk about "what a good kid I was" and "how beautifully I danced." I rehearsed early in the morning, before most people worked, and I'd know the latest dance moves, especially the latest fad—breakdancing. I was perfecting moves and then adding my own flavor to them. My schedule was simple—wake up, rehearse, go to school, rehearsal, eat, and go to bed. I was so motivated. So much so that I'd skip school just to rehearse more by myself. The obsession kept me from thinking about Mama being gone. And time went faster if I just kept working. She'd be back any day now I'd tell myself. Although, down deep inside, I knew the horrible truth.

By the time I was twelve, I was transferred from the local CYO group to a group in West Roxbury. This neighborhood was where all the rich White kids lived. All of them lived in pretty houses with moms and dads who had cars and most of them had a cat or dog. The perfect white picket fence thing. I was the only Black/Latina kid for sure, but I was so happy to be with this group because where I had been was nothing compared to this drill team (Winter Guard). This team competed. And they won trophies. And they got to travel and were pretty well known.

If I wasn't at school, I was rehearsing at home, or at the gym at a scheduled practice. I never talked much about my mother's death, but it was so recent and so in the air that I felt like I walked around with an additional notice on my head. The family-less kid. The parentless kid. The orphan. On top of being called names behind my back because of my skin color and my talent, I also had to listen to whispers about my new parentless status. I tried not to care. Auditions were set up to find a new captain for the junior drill team and I was determined to win.

The organization never mentioned what the audition would entail, but had told us to be prepared. I had been rehearsing and competing with the group for quite some time at this point and had made some friends but, at the end of the day, I always felt like the outsider. The Black girl from JP. Jamaica *Spain*. My quietness, my fear, was interpreted by most of the girls to be snobbery. They all thought that I thought I was better than all of them. I was. But it was because I worked twice as hard. They all hated me.

The few friends I had made were Mrs. Connelly's kids, and a couple of other girls who had gone to the same school as I did. Laura would become one of my best friends during that time. She lived in the same neighborhood I did, but over on the White side. Her mom and dad took a special interest in me early on when I performed at the local church. It was her dad who had taken my very first boots and gotten them cut for me when they were too long and Mama hadn't had enough money to get them taken care of. He had cleaned the blood off my little legs, and it was Laura's mom, Mrs. Dahl, who had bandaged me up. They would always be my ride to and from rehearsals. And sometimes Laura and I would rehearse together. Looking back, I believe they were the ones who had gotten me noticed and moved over to the West Roxbury group. When I was with them, I felt like I belonged. The Dahls would be one of the first families to take me in after Mama died. I would always be so grateful to them for so many reasons.

On the day of the audition so many things loomed over me. I knew in my heart that I had come up with a routine that was sure to be brilliant. I just needed to figure out one part and stop dropping the rifle after passing it through my right leg. I had picked this slow song from the movie *Fame*, "Out Here On My Own," performed by Irene Cara, for my audition. It was perfect. Everyone would expect a fast-paced song, because that would be easier, but I picked this song because it made so much sense. I worked so hard on my piece and hit myself so many times that eventually there were bruises all over my legs. During rehearsals I dropped the rifle plenty of times. I hit myself more often than not trying out new moves. At one point there was a bruise as big as a baseball on the inside part of my right leg. I had marks all over me, but that one would prove problematic. Regardless, I considered it a battle wound. Once I perfected my latest trick, and finalized the last choreographed pose, ultimately, all of it would prove to be worth it. I was ready.

The day of the audition everyone was nervous. I was extremely nervous, but I would not show it, I just couldn't. Mama had taught me early on that no matter how poor we were, no one ever needed to know it, so that's why we learn to behave appropriately and have manners. Proper etiquette. And somehow I interpreted that to mean, no matter how you're ever feeling, you have the ability to present something else if it will get you to the next step. And so I contained my feelings of nervousness pretty easily. By the time I was at the gym hall where we rehearsed, I was done practicing. Instead, I sat in the corner waiting my turn, watching everyone "warming up." I said my prayer and waited quietly in the corner, not letting fear overtake me.

My name was called. I was next. I picked up my rifle and walked into the second gym where six people sat along a table facing the stage. Of course, I knew all of them. The most important person to impress was Jarrod. He was the director and head instructor, and would most likely have the deciding vote. I put my cassette tape on the desk with my music so that I could perform. I started to walk back to the center of the stage to begin, and, as I did, one of the other judges, Sarah, the Captain of the Senior Corp, called out, "Carmen, what's this?"

I turned around. "My music for my audition," I replied. And everyone in the room laughed. I looked down at the floor a bit confused. I was feeling stupid. I said in my stutter, "W…W…Well, I can do it without the music too." And they laughed even louder.

One of the other judges, the manager of the Winter Guard, pulled out a cigarette and lit it as he put his feet up on the desk. Another judge, an alumnus of the program, started writing something in a notebook. Clearly, no one was at all interested in what I was about to do.

I stood up on the stage for what felt like forever, staring in confusion at all of them.

Finally Jarrod noticed that I was serious. He cleared his throat and made his way towards the stage. He said, "Carmen, you're going to be captain. It's not a question. We just had to put the audition together to make everyone feel like they had a chance. You don't have to audition, sweetie. We've all agreed you're the one."

"But I put together a routine. I rehearsed," I almost whispered.

"I know you did, doll, but you can just rest for a little bit right now. You've been through so much. Take a break. You don't have to do anything at all. We'll just all sit here for a little bit and then we'll call in someone else."

He jumped off the stage and went back and sat on the table and continued talking to the other judges. I was fuming. I was breathing through my nose so hard, my chest expanding with every deep breath.

"I don't want to be captain just because my mother died and I don't have anyone!" I screamed.

They all stopped talking and looked up at the stage in shock. It was the first time anyone had heard me raise my voice.

Jarrod stood up. "No one's making you captain because your mother died—"

I cut him off, "You just feel sorry for me. You all just feel sorry for me! I rehearsed. I came up with a routine. I want to show you. Please!"

And Jarrod put out his cigarette. He looked over at Sarah and motioned to her. She took the tape and put it in the recorder. The music started and I performed my heart out, dancing every moment and spinning my rifle and looking into the shadowy cars that had now become thousands of people. I was back on my street, under the light post. It was all so familiar. So comfortable.

The music stopped. I was frozen in my last pose. I was staring upward into the high ceiling. I was fiercely happy inside with my performance and I didn't miss the part through my legs. They clapped. They kept clapping. They stood up. Sarah came up on the stage and hugged me, then kissed me on the head. "You're quite something, little one. I better be careful or you'll be taking over my spot in the Senior Corp." I smiled and hugged her back hard.

Jarrod came over to me and grabbed my chin. "This is why I'm making you captain. Not because your mother died, but because you have such heart. I'm proud of you. And I know your mom is too." He then noticed the bruises on my legs. He turned me around and looked at my arms. Sarah was looking at my bruised body too.

"It's from trying to do tricks. I…I…I keep missing and hitting myself," I said, embarrassed.

"Okay. I could see that," he said, suspiciously. "But how about from now on if we get you some padding? If you're going to rehearse outside of hours, you let me know first and maybe either I or someone else can coach you? And I want you wearing protective gear, maybe even a helmet. I don't want you hitting your head learning those tricks, okay?"

"Um, okay," I said excitedly.

Sarah added, "And I'll give you some of my old padding so you can still work at home, okay? You can't be having all those bruises on your body when you perform."

"Really?" I was over the moon.

"Yes. Really." She hugged me again.

What I didn't realize until many years later was Jarrod had suspected that someone might be abusing me. So he began monitoring me as best he could along with enlisting a lot of the other mothers in the organization. I was never physically abused by anyone. Well, not repeatedly, anyways. But unbeknownst to me at the time, people were always looking out for me just to make sure.

Mama would have been proud of me for sure that day. Not because I became captain, but because I earned it.

As promised, I did get to work with Sarah and Jarrod alone. Sometimes wearing a football helmet, I'd attempt newer tricks with the rifle, and I'd bring with me the latest dance move (breakdancing) to any rehearsal that I could. Eventually, as a group, we'd compete. We won so many competitions it was amazing. Local awards mostly, but to me it might as well have been the world! But as much as I enjoyed competing with the drill team, my favorite was competing solo. Jarrod would take me on the weekends that we weren't competing as a group to these solo competitions. I'd get to compete by myself, but even more fascinating to me was getting to watch some of the greatest perform. I was twelve years old and competing against much older people. Although I never won any of those competitions, in a lot of ways, just being there, the only Black/Latina kid, the youngest, fiercely making the top twenty and then the top ten—that was winning enough!

Jarrod was the first person to acknowledge and reward my talent. He pushed me hard and let me try anything and everything. And for that, I will always consider him the best coach I ever had. But for secretly watching over me, protecting me, making sure I wasn't getting abused...well, for that I'll always be grateful.

* * *

I think I was trying so hard to get my footing in this new life that you just never occurred to me. I was missing Mama so much at times that my belly would ache and my chest would hurt. I didn't want to talk about it. Mama would be back. I was a loner. I was growing angry keeping all of it inside. Sometimes, when I was by myself, I'd have a good cry and I'd be fine. But those who knew me, who really knew me and loved me anyways—they could see where I was headed.

Mac

My seventh-grade teacher was named Mr. McAdams. Mr. Al McAdams. He always treated me kindly, maybe even specially.

One day, when I was sitting in the schoolyard having a hard time of it, he asked me if I wanted to head on over with him to a meeting. He promised me it would be quite boring, but at least I would have somewhere to go and "maybe afterwards we could grab a burger." I shrugged my shoulders and went along.

When we got there, he grabbed a coffee, handed me a soda, and told me to just sit in the back. He went and sat up front. There were lots of people there. No one I knew, of course, and no one my age. Everybody was older, like Mr. McAdams. And when the meeting started and the boring business stuff was out of the way, Mr. McAdams got up at the front of the group and began, "Hi, my name is Al and I'm an alcoholic."

I sat there riveted. The story he told about how he started drinking, getting his first taste from his dad's beer when he was just a little boy, to how his drinking almost killed him, to how he put his life back together again, was fascinating to me. Not so much the story, though it was remarkable, but that he let me, one of his students, hear it.

After the meeting, I waited by the door as Mr. McAdams made his way towards me.

"Ready to go?" he asked, almost pleased with himself.

"Uh huh," I said.

We ate dinner that night and talked briefly about AA, Alcoholics Anonymous. We talked more about what I was doing, where I was staying and if I needed anything at all, even money.

I was thrown just a bit. It was my teacher. But I just said I was fine and thanked him for the burger.

He gave me his home phone number and home address and told me, if I was ever in trouble or just needed someone to talk to, I could call him and he'd help as best he could. He also slipped in that I was always welcome to those Thursday night meetings if I ever wanted to just come in for a free soda and donuts.

"Um. Yeah. Thanks, but no thanks," was pretty much all I said. And he drove me to where I was staying that night.

I went to meetings pretty regularly after that. Sometimes with Al and sometimes not. If I was going by myself and couldn't go to an AA meeting, I'd catch a different meeting or an Al-Anon meeting. At first I started going because I had nowhere else to go. It was an easy way to stay out of the cold and get some free food.

But the therapy part of it seeped on through. The faith part too. And Mr. McAdams knew that all along. He'd give me little trinkets with sayings on them, or prayer booklets to look at—all to keep me motivated or interested, I suppose. It worked.

I wasn't an alcoholic but I met so many people in heartache. They'd been sober for years and gotten their life together and then they'd fall off the wagon and drink again. Their families would leave them, they'd lose everything and yet, they always could find their way back, pull themselves through. At the very least, they had faith. Not just in God, but in themselves. They inspired me. And they made me remember that I was never alone.

* * *

One specific Thursday night meeting I heard a man tell a story of how he had drunk himself into oblivion. He had lost his whole family. They no longer wanted anything to do with him. He hadn't seen his wife, or his ex-wife in years, and his children had grown up without him.

I wondered if maybe that's what had happened to you. That maybe you were just a drunk and Mama had pushed you out for the safety of our home. It made sense. Mama would have protected me like that. And the only reason why she never told me about you is because I would have been disappointed by what you really were: a drunk.

Jackson

The hard truth was, most days, I was on my own.

People in my mother's home were fighting over her belongings. Her house, ironically, was something she was in the process of buying. When she died, she owned it outright. Some agreement with the bank that if she died she owned it—or something like that. I didn't understand any of it back then but considering Mama was a housekeeper, so sickly and just barely getting by, it was quite an accomplishment trying to buy a house. She didn't leave a will, that wasn't the norm back then, at least for most people, so the house and Mama's other small belongings brought out the ugly in a lot of folk. I just wanted to get away from it all and stay away from them, so I'd spend most of my time rehearsing if I could.

Most days, no one knew where I was. I'd run away or stay away for long periods of time, sleeping at people's houses, and hanging out on the streets. As long as I went to school and went to rehearsal, no one seemed to mind. Or maybe no one seemed to notice. Sometimes I just felt like no one really cared.

The first person I remember saving me was this guy named Jackson. I was still just about twelve years old at the time and walking home from hanging on Forbes Street. It was two in the morning and I decided to make my trek home, a very common occurrence back in the day.

I said goodnight to everyone on the stoop and started on my way. Maybe if I walked quickly I could make it home in half an hour, I thought to myself.

It was a cold night. I remember it clearly. There wasn't any snow, but I could see the dark sky. I couldn't see any stars, but I imagined them up above the city lights gleaming down anyways. There weren't any cars or movement on the street, which made it so quiet, and somehow so very peaceful. It felt like I was the only person in the world and that it all belonged to me. I was a happy little girl walking home that night. I wondered if my footsteps on the concrete were really as loud as they seemed in the quiet still air.

I came up towards the middle school; the fence to the schoolyard lined that part of the street. A car flashed by. I kept walking and didn't think anything of it. I noticed it stopped a ways ahead of me.

I straightened up, kept my head forward, and walked at a steady pace.

The car then turned around and was heading back. It slowed as it got closer.

I kept walking.

The same faded-black car then passed on over the center divider and headed directly towards me.

It stopped. And as I passed the car, I heard another come from behind. Without turning my head, I continued on. I tried to stand tall. I was so little, but I had to be tough. I continued looking forward and kept on walking as if the cars didn't exist. Show no fear. No fear.

Another car, a red-mustard-colored one, jumped the sidewalk and was now in front of me. I stopped. I wanted to take a deep breath, but couldn't. My throat felt solid. No air was getting through. The car lights blinked twice. I heard the doors open and shut on either side. My heart pounded so hard it echoed through my ears. The car behind me slowly made its way closer. Its lights shined so brilliantly. Shadowy figures walked along towards me. I hadn't noticed but I had been slowly backing up. I hit the fence. They had me cornered. There was nowhere for me to go.

One by one, they walked towards me. A few more got out of the cars. I remember thinking, how many? Where did they come from? Someone from the back was calling me "chica-linda." Another was calling me "whore."

I knew what was about to happen. Well, I thought I knew. I was only twelve and a half years old, still a virgin, so I wasn't very sure, but I knew I would die that day. I remembered thinking how glad I was it wasn't snowing. I counted seven. One was smoking. There was a stench of beer, pot, and cigarettes, and whatever else they had been into. The first guy, the one that called me chica, came up to me and grabbed my bag. He threw it to the ground and licked my face. I gagged. He grabbed my throat with one hand. He told me that I should be afraid. That I was a stupid little bitch for walking home alone. That maybe I wanted it. I heard someone else laugh from the back. Then I heard someone opening a can of something. My throat was so dry.

He stopped choking me, but kept his hand at my throat. His other hand stroked my hair. His breath stank. Another guy touched the small of my back and dared me to look his way. The one in front unzipped his pants. Another took off his belt and yelled, "Let's tie the bitch up."

Someone was trying to unbutton my jeans. I could feel his rings against my skin as he undid the top button. I would have tried to fight, but there were so many and I could see the blade from the corner of my eye. My shirt had already been ripped open. It was so cold. I could taste the salt from my tears…

I got slapped more than once because I wouldn't talk. He wanted me to say all sorts of things—it was a game to them. Instead, I stayed stoic, tears streaming down my face. I just stared, motionless, my pants at my ankles. And, just as the first guy was about to pull down my underwear, something lifted him clear off the ground and away from me. He landed near the car door with a loud thump. At the same time, the one who kept calling me "whore" keeled over from being cracked in the back of the knees with what seemed to be a bat. I fell to the ground, scrambling to pull my pants back over my underwear. I huddled next to the fence, grabbing what little was left of my shirt. Blood was everywhere. I couldn't remember how my coat had been taken off. Where was it? I looked across the way and two guys lay on the ground, beaten to a pulp. I grabbed for my bag to the left and saw another man gasping for breath as someone kicked him one more time in the gut to make sure he was out cold.

I stayed against the fence, shaking from fear and the cold, buckets of tears rolling down my face. I couldn't control myself any longer at all.

I didn't move from that spot. I clung to the fence for dear life, just barely hanging on.

A shadowy figure walked over to me. The lights still beamed from behind, but I could see it was someone familiar. It was Jackson. He cleaned his bloodied hands on the end of his white T-shirt and pulled me up. Most of my shirt and bra had been torn and one of the other boys took off his jacket and handed it to Jackson, who wrapped me in it. He wiped my tears with his sleeve, grabbed my face and looked closely—first the left side, then the right. He looked at my head; I'd been cut above the eye. He asked me if I was hurt anywhere else. I shook my head no. He told me to get my things and to "get my ass in the car." That he didn't want to hear a word from me. "Not a muther-fucking word, do you hear me?" I nodded.

I sat in that car for what seemed to be hours. I noticed a slice on my leg and a gash on my arm, but nothing major. The bleeding stopped. Jackson and his friends finished off their "discussions" with the other gang. I could hear Jackson telling them that if he ever found out that any girls in his neighborhood were touched by anyone, he'd personally take care of the situation himself. He then told them, "And that's my little sister. Don't ever even look at her. Do you hear me?" And I could hear a muffled and very stressed yes come out of one of their mouths. I didn't dare look.

When Jackson and the rest of his crew got back to their cars, they had blood all over them. Jackson came over and told me to get out of the passenger seat and get in back. He told Armand to drive and he sat in the back with me. When the car backed up, I saw the boys that tried to hurt me laying all over the street and sidewalk. They were moving around, but still seemingly in pain and trying to get up. As I continued to look out the window, Jackson looked at me and said, "What do you have to say for yourself?" He was still so pumped up and on edge from attacking the gang.

I leaned back. But I didn't say a word. I kept looking down at my hands.

He grabbed my face towards his and yelled, "When I ask you a fucking question, you answer me!"

"I'm sorry," I said in between gasps.

"You better be. And I better never find out that you ever walked home alone again. Do you hear me?"

"Yes."

"Alright then. I'm taking you home. Why you still crying? You said nothing was wrong with you. Did they hurt you? If they did, don't worry, we got them good."

Armand and Rocko chimed in from the front seat, laughing and being so proud of themselves. "We fucked them up good…"

When the car finally stopped in front of the house, Jackson asked me one more time what was wrong. I looked at him for a long time and then said, "Nothin.'" After a few more seconds of him staring at me I blurted out, "You called me your little sister."

"Yeah, well, so what?"

"Well, I'm not. I mean, you're…White and I'm…not."

"You are Carmencita. You're my little sister. I used to change your diapers for goodness sake."

I looked at him bewildered at first, and then I saw the smirk on his face and couldn't help myself from blurting out loud, "No you didn't!"

He laughed a hearty laugh. "Yeah, I did." And then seriously he said, "If anyone ever asks. You got that? This is familia. We take care of our own. And now that your mom is gone, well…"

"Well, what?"

"Nevermind. Get your ass inside and I never want to talk about this ever again. You understand me?"

"Yeah. Okay."

I stepped out of the car. Behind Jackson's car were six other vehicles. All of his boys. They'd gotten out of their cars too as if to all watch me personally make it to the door. I started to take off the jacket that was loaned to me, covered in blood, and Rocko said, "Keep it. You'll give it to me some other time, okay?" I bowed my head in agreement and walked up the stairs to the porch. My hands were shaking as I found the key in the bottom of my bag—it felt like it took forever to find the lock, but finally I did. And once inside, I heard the cars start up and leave.

That was the day Jackson and his crew saved me. A mixture of White, Black, and Latino kids whose common bond was the streets. They were the good guys. Had I been raped, it would have changed my life forever. But the gift Jackson gave me was far greater than anyone could have ever imagined. A sense of family. The idea that I mattered, that I was worth protecting. That I belonged. And throughout my teen years it was partially living up to Jackson's expectations that kept me going when I was running the streets after Mama died. No one messed with Jackson or anyone in his crew. And he said I was his "little sister." I was so proud to be considered that special. It meant so much to me back then.

It still does.

* * *

I fantasized so much as a little girl. If Jackson was my big brother, then Jackson was just like his dad. And "Papi" or you had to be all the good things Jackson was. Jackson wasn't a drunk and if he did drink, he could handle it. Jackson was a man and protected his family. Jackson had a crew. People followed him, admired him. Jackson was a hero. And I wanted a hero for a dad.

Some days I'd feel guilty for even spending any time thinking about you at all. I was losing memories of Mama. I'd recite things in my head as much as possible, Johnny Carson, know who you really are, television isn't a toy, etiquette, dignity, don't lie, cheat, what else? What did I forget? Her smile. The twinkle in her eyes...

Marcus

I had been court ordered to attend a day camp at Boston College the following summer. That's what I was told anyways.

I don't remember too many times when I'd screamed at anyone as a kid, but when I was told I had no choice, I did exactly that. All I wanted to do was hang on Forbes, dance, and go to drill team practice. I didn't want anything else. It was bad enough I felt obligated to go to AA meetings now, but still, it was my choice. And yet, even though I was a good kid who stayed out of trouble, I was pulled out of all my activities and walked to the place where the school bus would pick me up for day camp! My guardians at the time wouldn't leave till they personally saw me get on the bus. I hated them.

And I was angry.

Mama had been dead almost a whole year, ten months to be exact, and she still hadn't returned. My world had changed. I never knew where I would be sleeping or when I would definitely eat, but the one constant, rehearsals, mornings and afternoons, was being ripped away from me. No questions asked. School was over for the summer. And somehow this stupid camp was what was "best for me." Hate was festering in my heart. Not sadness or disappointment, but hate.

I walked on the bus and didn't look at anybody. I sat in an empty seat and stared out the window. My memory went back to that day Mama and I had taken the trolley and then the many buses to get my boots. My horseback-riding boots. I watched as all the pretty houses passed on by and wished that I could go back. I wished she'd come back.

My head was leaning against the glass window and when the bus went over a huge bump my head slammed against it. It hurt so bad but it was just as well. I didn't care and I didn't flinch. Somehow the pain felt good. Immediately one of the camp counselors on the bus, this really pretty, dainty, skinny woman with long, straight, perfect hair and perfect teeth, came over to me and asked if I was okay. I slowly turned my head. I gave her a once-over and just stared blankly through her. I didn't care what she was asking me. I wanted to go home. Back to the gym. And she could feel the hate piercing through my eyes. To my surprise, she backed away slowly. She must have feared I was one of those gangster kids who carried a blade or something. Typical White girl. But I was glad. She was afraid. I looked back out the window, making my plans to slip away once the bus stopped wherever the bus was finally heading. Clearly, Marcia Brady over there wasn't going to do anything to stop me. And this time, I'd run away for good.

When the bus stopped in the parking lot of the Boston College grounds right outside the stadium, I waited as all the kids rushed to get off the bus. It was obvious they'd all been there before and were excited to be back at "camp." I was sure it couldn't possibly be anything compared to dancing or Winter Guard at all. It probably didn't even hold a candle to hanging in the Boston Common watching the latest breakdancers do their thing. I watched out the window as they all jumped off the bus and the counselors got them all lined up like little robots in a straight line. And then, slowly, I slid under the seat so that no one would see me in the window and force me outside. Once the bus driver left and locked the bus, I'd make my get away. They wouldn't even notice.

I waited a bit. When I could hardly hear the voices of all the campers, I got up from underneath the chair and started to make my way toward the front of the bus. Just then, a man popped up a few rows ahead, scaring me. He said, "Hey there. Ready to go?"

"Wh…wh…what?"

"Aaah, you stutter. Good to know. Let me write that down." He pulled out a clipboard and started writing.

"I..I…I don't stutter."

He smiled. "I kinda think you do." He said it without looking at me and almost laughing. I hated him. I hated him right then and there.

"What were you planning? Running away?" He was now serious and staring right at me.

I didn't say anything at all. I was hard again. Cold. Hoping my stare would scare him too, just like it had scared little Marcia Brady. But he didn't budge.

I kept staring. He was easily Italian. His skin was darker than mine; he had thick, dark-brown, straight hair that fell into his eyes. He shook his head to clear his long bangs from his face. He was really muscular and, well, obviously way taller than me. Even though his body was massive and he could easily hurt me, there was a kindness to him. A jokiness in his tone. But I still hated him.

He asked again, "Do…you…want…to…run…away?"

"Yes!" I screamed out loud.

"Good. That's a start. Where would you go?"

I didn't say anything at all. I hadn't really thought that far yet.

"Is it customary to ask you a question twice before you answer?" He then said it more sternly and again very slowly, "Where…would…you…go?"

"I…I…I d…d…don't know!" I was now afraid of him.

"Well, that's pretty stupid. You don't have a plan? I figured you were a little smarter than that, being that you're from JP and all."

I couldn't believe he was talking to me this way. I was breathing deeply. My mouth clenched, my eyes glaring. I was ready to fight. I said nothing.

He didn't care about my changed demeanor; he continued on without looking at me but staring out the bus. "Well, if you stayed, you could eat something, maybe go swimming, meet some other people, play basketball. Who knows, you might even like it."

"I…I…I'm not gonna like it," I said as fiercely as I could.

"How do you know?" He started walking up the isle towards me.

"I just do!" I screamed. "Stay away from me! Stay away from me!"

He got closer. "How about if you just give it a try, just one day? Can you do that for me?"

"Nnnnooo! I hate you! I hate all of you! Stay away from me!" I started to punch him in the torso, I kicked him in the leg, and he stood there, letting me. I kept screaming at him, my fists trying hard to hurt him, but I was just hurting myself.

Finally he grabbed me and pulled me up over the rows of seats and carried me to the front of the bus, all along as I continued trying to hit him. He sat me in the first row of the bus and put me in his lap and held me close as I kept trying to fight him. I'd exhausted so much energy I just couldn't fight anymore. And as he kept bear hugging me, I cried. I cried so hard. Harder than I'd ever cried before. I cried because I was angry. I cried for Mama. I cried because I was alone. I cried because I didn't have a plan. I cried because I had nowhere to go.

I started hyperventilating. He rubbed my back so I would calm down. He kept saying, "It's gonna be alright. I promise you, it's gonna be alright."

I finally realized I had been crying into his shirt and pulled away. I sat next to him on the seat. I looked up at him. He smiled and kept looking forward.

"I'm sorry," I said meekly.

"No problem. It's what I'm here for." He winked.

We sat in silence for a bit, then Barbie, aka Marcia Brady, made her way back to the bus.

She opened the door and walked halfway up the steps when he called out to her. "We're fine. Me and Carmen are going to skip morning call and we'll meet you guys for lunch." He looked at me as if to ask if that was okay, and I nodded in agreement.

"Um, okay, Marcus. I'll see you guys later." And Barbie pranced off the bus.

We sat there in silence again. I was feeling sad and plenty exhausted. I wasn't sure what to do and then he broke the silence. "I'm Marcus. Quarterback for the Boston College Eagles and your very own camp counselor for the summer."

"*Football?*" I said, like it was stupid.

"Yeah, what's wrong with that?"

"Nut-tin'. You don't look fat enough to be a football player." I laughed.

He chided back, "First of all, it's 'noth*in*G.' There's a G at the end of that word. And second, I'm a quarterback. And quarterbacks aren't fat. You know a lot about football, huh?"

I busted up laughing. "Um, no. Noth*in*G at all." I emphasized the G sound.

"Aaah, much better." He smiled back. "Whattayah say? Give camp a try? Just give it one week. If you don't like it, I'll help you run away. Deal?"

"You know I don't have a choice. I have to be here."

"Not true. You always have a choice. And I don't know," he said matter-of-factly.

"What do you mean, you don't know? Why did you wait for me then? You must know all about me. You knew my name. You knew I was gonna run away. I bet they told you everything…" I was getting upset again.

He leaned forward and put his big arms on the divider. "C, I don't know anything about you except your name, age, and the bus stop we'd be picking you up at and dropping you off at. But you walked on sad. You didn't say goodbye to the people you were with, and you didn't look at anyone on the bus. It wasn't that hard to figure out. I could just tell you didn't want to be here."

"So what?" I said under my breath.

"So…" He cleared his throat. "Maybe I know what that feels like. Maybe you and I aren't so different. And maybe, just maybe, I can help you stop feeling so defensive. It's not just you against the world, you know."

I didn't say anything. I looked over at him as he stared away from me again. He said, "So, whattya say? Give me one week?"

"Yeah, yeah, yeah. Okay. One week," I said reluctantly.

"What you meant to say was 'Yes, Marcus, I would be happy to try camp for one week,'" he corrected me.

"Yeah, if I was one of your White rich campers, that's exactly what I wouldda said."

He started laughing and got up. "Okay. I see I got a smart aleck on my hands. Let's go see if we can still grab some breakfast, okay?"

"Marcus? Can I ask you a question first?"

"Sure. Shoot."

"You said we weren't that different, but you don't know me. How do you know we're the same?"

"Look, it's tough being a kid. I was a kid once. So I know. And I bet you've got some battle wounds, just like I did. But if you let someone who's already been there help you out, well, it might be a little easier. Capiche?"

"Yes, kapeesh." I giggled because I knew it sounded all wrong coming out of my mouth.

I got up off the chair, wiped my face with the back of my hand, and we both walked off the bus together.

That summer I was attached at the hip to Marcus. I ran track, played basketball, learned how to swim (for real), did all sorts of arts and crafts, and even won Most Valuable Player on the basketball team. Then, I also won the biggest prize, Best Camper of the Year. And Marcus secretly cheered me on every step of the way.

After camp ended that summer, Marcus kept in touch with me, or at least he tried to. He got me tickets to the games and I'd go with a friend, usually with Mr. McAdams, my teacher from school, my AA buddy, and we'd cheer him on playing. The following summer I went back to Boston College's camp because I wanted to, not because I was ordered to. And Marcus was there again, being the great camp counselor he was to everyone.

I still ran away from home a lot. But sometimes I'd run to Boston College and Marcus would find me and get me back on track. He never pressured me, but always let me vent my problems out, and then we'd walk through them together. He never told me what to do directly, he just kept asking me questions. He was like a good older brother to me that way. He taught me to stop keeping things bundled up inside. Most times, when I'd stop on by if he had time, we'd play basketball, or just talk. Most times I just needed to talk to someone. And Marcus would be there for me. And he'd remind me, "Never be afraid. Let what's aching inside, out. If we don't let the pain out, then the wound never gets to heal."

"That sounds like something Mama would say," I told him as I sat on his dorm room floor one night.

"Of course it's something your mother would say. Who do you think told me to tell you?" He'd wink and give a great big smile, and somehow I kinda felt like maybe he really did have a touch of Mama in him.

* * *

I'd sit in the stands sometimes and wonder if you liked football. There'd be so many fathers with their kids in the stands, wearing their jerseys, and a flash of "going to the game with Papi" would come over me.

If you knew me at all, I wondered if you were worried about where I'd end up. Maybe you had no idea that Mama was pregnant after all. Maybe she never told you. Maybe she was waiting to tell you when I turned sixteen.

Charlie

It was perfect.

Beautiful trees, flowers, all sorts of nature, and yet, the brilliance of the city all around. Whenever I was there, I just felt happy. Maybe it was watching the kids play in the fountain at the frog pond with their parents, or looking at the Swan Boats cross along the water, I'm not sure. But when I needed to be alone, away from all the craziness, the Boston Common is where I'd go.

During midday, businesspeople would go back and forth to meetings, eat lunch, or just sit on a bench and read the paper. Tourists would walk along taking in the

71

sights and watching artists sketch a drawing or a mime walk an imaginary ladder. Breakdancers performed for crowds and some folk just begged for money. Sometimes, if I was really up for it, I'd challenge a fellow breakdancers just for kicks. I wasn't as good of a breakdancer as I was just a dancer, but I could certainly hold my own.

The "combat zone," Boston's downtown seedy side, was also not too far away. "Ladies of the night" would work their magic and be seen hanging with their pimps or chatting up drug dealers during the daylight hours. Homeless men would stake out an area, at least until police herded them away. Every class and color converged in this one beautiful space. And though there were so many people around, when I was there sitting on my favorite bench, somehow I always felt relieved, alone and at some sort of peace.

One late afternoon I accidentally fell asleep on my favorite bench. When I woke, I was disoriented. It was night. My body, though once comfortable, was now achy and feeling the chilly air. I'd been stretched out fully along the green wooden splintered slabs, unsure for how long exactly, and my body was now feeling the pain.

I rubbed my eyes and noticed my papers and books along the ground. I'd been working on my homework, but obviously had fallen asleep midway. I had stayed in one position for too long and I was hurting. I attempted to turn over, and as I did, I looked up and at the foot of the bench I saw a man standing perfectly still.

I froze. No breath. I couldn't breathe. I swallowed so hard; the sound seemed to echo in the dark empty night. He was facing me. The light from behind cast him in shadow. I couldn't see his face. He didn't move. For half a second, I thought I had sat next to a statue, on the wrong bench, but then I saw slight movement and fear, sheer panic, set in.

With a knot in my throat and my heart thumping loudly, I managed a hollow and pained, "What do you want?" But he said nothing. He didn't move. I could feel the cramp in my spine. Slowly, carefully, I shifted my legs off the bench. Immediately, he leaned forward and grabbed the back of the bench.

My heart raced even more. I jumped off the bench ready to run and, as I attempted to grab my bag, I noticed he sat down. He sat down at the end of the bench. I was scared, but more confused. He didn't say a word. He was stoic sitting there, looking straight ahead. It was like the statue had now sat down.

Puzzled, I said out loud, "You... just wanted to sit down? But there's an empty bench over there. There's a...bunch of them." The words came out too fast to take them back and I realized this man could kill me, what was I thinking? I should be running. And then his head turned slowly towards me and, with a crooked smirk, and without saying a word, I knew exactly what he was thinking: this was his bench, not mine.

I shook my head just a bit. "I'm sorry. I didn't know." And his head turned back to look forward again as he seemed to wait for me to leave.

Feeling less afraid, I tied my sneaker. I finished gathering the rest of my things and looked through my bookbag for my transfer ticket for the trolley. I pulled out a bag of Cheetos. I opened them and started to eat a couple when the statuesque man looked over and eyed the bag in my hand. I asked him if he wanted some but he didn't respond.

So, before making my way over to the trolley stop, I crumpled closed the bag of Cheetos and put it on the bench a little closer to him. As I walked away from my newfound friend, I heard clearly the leftover bag of Cheetos opening. I smiled and made my way into the subway.

I would come every so often to the park, usually running away from the chaos that was my life at the time, and, in a short period of time, me and the statuesque man developed a kind of system or rhythm to our visits. I would sit on the bench doing my homework or whatever, and when he showed up I'd take out the food I'd stolen from whomever's house I'd been staying at the night before. He never said a word to me, but we had conversations nonetheless.

At some point I named him Charlie. He seemed like a Charlie and it was the first thing that popped into my head one day when I asked him what his name was. Of course, he never uttered a sound, but he answered to it, so it worked out just fine.

I couldn't tell how old Charlie was, but his eyes were that pretty, cheery blue that almost smiled and twinkled even if he wasn't trying. He seemed tired most days, maybe even sad. And he was definitely old. His face was so dirty, but it almost looked like the black camouflage makeup soldiers wear when in combat. I asked him once if he'd been in the war and, although he never answered, I swear his blue eyes dimmed for just a sec. His clothes were army-like, though he wore so many layers I couldn't really tell how big or small he was. His gloves had the tips cut off, and the shoes he wore—heavy, black combat boots. Probably the cleanest thing on him.

Every few days or so, I'd come by and sit on our bench, and I'd always try to bring enough food for both of us. I'd bring enough for that day's meal and always try to bring a few more items for Charlie to take with him. Bologna and cheese sandwiches with mustard on Wonder Bread seemed to be one of his favorites. He was always grateful, and gave me that smirky half-grin I'd gotten used to that clearly meant "Thank you so much."

Some nights, when I couldn't go home or just wouldn't make myself go home, I'd sleep on that bench. And Charlie would stand watch, just like the first day we met. I'd bring him food, and he'd stand guard while I slept. It was our unspoken deal.

And then one day he didn't show up. I knew something was off, but I wanted to give him the food I'd brought. Right before nightfall, I trekked over to Charlie's shack, which really consisted of a few cardboard boxes meshed together with a tin-looking roof of some sort. I knew where it was, of course—not because I had ever been invited, but because at times I'd seen him walking towards his place to bring back the bag of food or goodies I might have given him.

When I opened the flap, there he was. Lying on the ground. Motionless. I laughed at first because I thought he might be joking. Pretending to be sleeping. But he didn't move. I poked his leg and something didn't feel right. I tried again. I grabbed his shiny boots with both hands and shook him harder but he didn't wake. It came to me in a rush—Charlie was dead.

My heart froze. I swear it felt like it stopped beating. And when it resumed, it was so loud I thought it would leap out of my chest. I was breathing heavy. Before I knew it I was running down the street. Running faster than I'd ever run before.

When I finally stopped, I didn't know where I was. I threw up in an alley and somehow started calming down. I sat down on the curb and cried some more. Under the light post in some fancy neighborhood, I watched the cars go back and forth for hours. Eventually, as the lamplight flickered on, I wiped my face, and made my way back home.

That was the first dead body I'd ever seen.

Mama died years ago. I always imagined, wished, she'd return. No one ever told me she died. But seeing Charlie that night, I knew she never could return.

I cried a lot for Charlie that night. But also, I finally cried for Mama.

* * *

You know, when I met Charlie I thought of you a lot. It was possible that you were a solider on leave who met Mama and, just maybe, had one beautiful night with her and had to leave the next day to serve our country. That always makes me smile. Or maybe you were Charlie. Somewhere lost and alone. If that were true, I'd surely never know.

When I was a little girl, I could make believe you were just about anyone. Chico, the bus driver who would take me to school when I was in the first grade, or the crossing guard with the smiley face who'd stop the traffic and help us walk on by. But never once had I thought about you being just as sick as Mama, or as lost as Charlie, or dead. It just never crossed my mind, until I knew and lost Charlie.

Francisco

I started working in a convenience store when I was about fifteen. I stocked shelves, moved boxes, but most times worked the cash register. It was my first job. Al, Mr. McAdams, my teacher, had gotten it for me. He knew the owners.

I was grateful, but still I hated it. It took away from my rehearsal time, but I needed the cash. Even if I wasn't paying for rent anywhere because I was lucky and living on different people's couches most days, it still helped with the little things I needed—from lunch to dancing tights and shoes, or sneakers, or a new rifle for Winter Guard practice. I also got to eat there. Junk food mostly, and maybe I should have paid, but, if no one was around, I didn't.

Mr. McAdams caught me stealing once. I was so embarrassed. Not that I was stealing, but that I got caught. It brought me back to the jawbreaker day at the grocery store with Mama. It's not that I didn't know stealing was a bad thing—of course I did—but it was just a few dollars

76

here and there. Mr. McAdams had come in to check on me and caught me right in the act. I had taken a few dollars out of the register and slipped them into my pocket. Busted. I promised I wouldn't do it again and I didn't do it again. He gave me another chance. Like Mama used to say, "If you're gonna lie, cheat, or steal, you better do it right or don't do it at all." Honestly though, I conveniently "forgot" the rest of the lesson and just got better at stealing... you know, if I needed to.

A lot of folk would come into that store. The same folk. Boring neighborhood old fogies mostly. But it was such an easy place to be, so whenever I did have to work, once I was there I didn't really mind it all that much. I would try and do my homework most nights, but I was always distracted by the music I'd keep on the radio. And, of course, rap was in its heyday, hitting the airwaves with the likes of the Sugarhill Gang blaring "Rappers Delight." I loved it. I knew every word. Disco was big back then too, and hip hop was king, and I'd jam right behind the counter, ignoring most folks who walked in the door if a good song was on.

I loved music. I loved that when I sang or rapped I didn't stutter. Yeah, I still stuttered, a lot. It started when I was a little kid. Really bad too. Mostly with sentences that started with a vowel. Or if I had to answer the phone and say "Hello" it would come out as "Eeee—eeee—llo." I had found a way around my stuttering problem most days, by just keeping my mouth shut. But when I was caught off guard, or if I had to do something I felt uncomfortable with, I'd stutter. And the thing about stuttering for me was, the moment I stuttered, the more I would continue to stutter and the worse it would get. It would sometimes get so bad that people would do the "kind" thing and finish the sentence for me. Somehow that was even more annoying.

It only got worse as I got older. More so after Mama died. But when music was on, I was inwardly relaxed and not focused on my speaking problem. It was another reason I listened to music so much. Yes, I was a dancer, disco was big, breakdancing was brilliant, and I was good at all of it. But there was also something calming about music for me. It relaxed me, made me calm. And usually, after listening to music, I could speak pretty easily.

One day a really tall older guy walked into the store with black greasy hair and a long, dark beard. I'd never seen him before and he reeked of cigarettes. He had a thin, brown lit cigarette dangling out of the side of his mouth. It was not a brand we carried in the store. Foreign. He came in, looked up strangely for a second, walked down the aisle grabbing a couple of bags of chips, and returned to the counter. He didn't look at me at all, just threw the bags up on the counter and went through his brown, old leather wallet that seemed like it was falling apart. I rang him up. "Fifty cents please." He threw a couple of coins on the counter, blew smoke out of the side of his mouth and nose—still not touching this filterless cigarette—and walked out the store, opening one of the bag of chips.

This became a pretty regular thing. He had most likely just moved to the neighborhood; sometimes he'd buy other things like beer or aspirin. But there wasn't a week he didn't come by without his dangling, smelly cigarette, his greasy hair and his falling-apart wallet. He kinda freaked me out a bit. But he seemed harmless enough.

Then one day, as he pulled out a dollar to pay for a bottle of orange soda, he asked me in this thick, deep accent, "Whath's jure name?"

"Excuse me?"

"Whath's jure name? Como te llamas."

"W-w-why?" I stuttered.

In the strangest, but most interesting Spanish I'd ever heard he said, "Because I'm asking. What is it with you Americans? Someone asks you a question, you should answer it, not ask a question back."

All of a sudden, what seemed like greasy hair and a long, dirty beard guy transformed right in front of me into a very distinguished man. If I had known the word eloquent back then, that's what I would have used to describe him. His hair wasn't greasy at all, but it was long and thinning. His beard was also long and perfectly manicured, if not just a bit too lengthy. His wallet wasn't a dirty, but a vintage brown leather case; now all I saw was a very old and extraordinarily intricate embroidered small satchel. He still hadn't looked at me.

"Um…My name is Carmen."

"Aaaah, tu nombre es Cahrmeng. That is a very beautiful name."

"Thanks. But it's just Car-men." I pronounced it in proper English for him.

He was looking straight at me with piercing brown eyes. "No, jure da one who say it wrong. It's Cahhhhhhrrrrmeng. It is a Spanish name." He continued on in Spanish, "You should be proud of your Spanish heritage. And you should speak Spanish all the time. From now on, when I come in here, you only speak to me in Spanish, okay? Everything."

I looked at him curiously. What an odd thing to say, but I was game. "Okay. But what's your name?"

"No te entiendo," he said devilishly. *I don't understand you.*

And in a very broken stutter Spanish I replied, "B-b-b-b-ien. Pero que es tu nombre?" *Okay, but what is your name?*

"Me llamo Francisco."

"Okay, got it. Francisco. Nice to meet you."

"No. En Español por favor. Yes, Fran-*thfis*-co."

And so it began. Every time Francisco came into the store, I'd do my best to talk to him in Spanish and he'd pretend to practice his English with me. His English was perfect but he'd pretend to struggle along to make me feel better about my horrible Spanish. I could understand it—even his Madrid Spain kind of Spanish, which in our neighborhood was considered very high brow. My neighborhood was filled with Puerto Ricans, Cubans, Dominicans, and Mama was originally from Honduras in Central America. I never knew any other people from Honduras, but I knew that's where I was from, or Mama actually. I was born in the US. I was Latina in the ways that mattered, but my Spanish was a mess. Broken. A mixture of different dialects covered and forever enveloped with a great heavy American accent. Francisco was just glad that I was trying. He thought if I'd just get better at speaking Spanish, I'd lose that American accent eventually. It's always good to hope.

It was a Thursday evening. Downpouring rain. Not a lot of people were coming into the store and it was dark and somewhat gloomy out. I sat at the cashier counter even bored with the music at this point, though I kept tapping along. I was done with my homework and watching the clock tick, tick, tick as slowly as possible, waiting for the shift to move on by. It was agonizing.

Then, three girls walked in. All a little older than me. I'd seen them before. Rich girls. The blonde hair, the Lacoste alligator shirts with the collars starched stiff, the name-brand jeans, the cool Nike sneakers. They rushed in with one umbrella, laughing and giggling, and then stood at the doorway inside the store as to not get wet. They didn't even notice me. They stood there, talking, laughing, acting as if this was their personal place to wait while the rain subsided. At first I thought I'd say nothing. It was raining after all, and they weren't really doing anything but being a little loud. Then one of the girls grabbed a pack of bubble gum off the shelf. She opened it and shared it with her two friends. She didn't even consider paying for it.

The next girl, another blonde (honestly, they all really did look exactly the same) went off and grabbed a soda from the fridge. She opened it with her own bottle opener, flicked the cap onto the floor, and started drinking it. On her way back she passed my counter, still with no consideration of paying. I had to say something.

And so they stood there. Talking. Giggling. Sharing. Laughing. Not once looking at me. And now, girl number three talked about wanting her own ginger ale. I had to stop this!

"I...I...I...I...I...I..." Nothing came out.

"What? Did you say something?" The girl had turned around, her hair flying perfectly in the air after her.

"Yyyyyou...need to pay for that!" I tried to cheat the words and raise my voice when it finally came out.

"What are you going to do if we don't?" she said, real sarcastically as if I were dumb. "Do you u-n-d-e-r-s-t-a-n-d me?" she squealed jokingly, using her fingers to pretend she was speaking sign language.

The other girls laughed out loud.

I was angry. I knew this was going to be a fight. One that I'd probably lose.

Blonde number two grabbed more stuff off the shelves and just started opening things one by one, dropping them on the floor. She stared at me while she did it, and the other two kept prodding me to "Try and talk," hoping I'd make an attempt and stutter more so they could make fun of me.

But anger trumps stuttering every time.

Blondie number two sat up on the shelf and knocked down the cans as she pretended to say "Sorry" in a very non-sorry way. My blood was boiling.

I slowly walked on over to my bookbag and grabbed my knife. If it was going to be three against one, I'd make it a fair fight. At the end of the day, I was just a girl from the 'hood, after all. A knife was standard. Something about cutting off a piece of that blonde hair made me feel good about the possibility. I was enraged.

Blonde girl number three, the bigger, thicker one, with the red lipstick asked, "What the hell are you doing on this side of town anyways? Don't all the spics live in Jamaica

Spain?" They all laughed. I made my move toward the flimsy gate from the counter space to the store floor. With my knife concealed in my right hand, tucked under my sleeve, I started to walk toward blonde number one.

From a distance we heard a sound. Someone walking from the back. A man with boxes came from the farthest aisle. At first I had no idea who it was since I was pretty sure no one was in the store earlier. It was Francisco. He put the boxes down, still with a lit brown cigarette in his mouth. He looked at me directly, as if to ask me if everything was okay.

The girls seemed to snap to attention. "Oh, Professor, what are you doing here?" Blonde girl number one asked, almost startled at who had just caught her. She jumped off the shelf and straightened herself.

And with his cool, thick, Spaniard-esque accent he said to her, "Jennifer, I live in this neighborhood, *Jamaica Plain."* He took in a long drag and blew it out through his nose and mouth at the same time. "And this is Carmen. A good friend who also minds my store. Now what are you girls doing way out here? Shouldn't you be somewhere near campus?"

In the sweetest voice Jennifer replied, "Oh, my dad is on his way to pick me up. Um, us up. We were eating at the pizza place, you know, The Same Old Place, and got caught in the rain. Carmen was cool enough to let us wait here." Blondie girl two cleared her throat and looked at me as if to beg I'd go along. I stood motionless, chin up, chest out, looking taller than I should be, more angry now at the lies. The knife still cuffed, the sharp blade hitting lightly against my skin. I didn't move. I'm not sure I even blinked.

"Well," Francisco garbled between drags. "Quite a mess here."

"Oh, yeah, my mistake," Jennifer said. "We'll pick it up, Professor."

Looking at me directly, the big blonde girl chimed in with fake sympathy, "We are so sorry, Carmen."

A car horn barked through the rain outside; it was Jennifer's dad. They quickly threw what little they had picked up onto the counter, half-apologized again, and nearly stumbled out the door. I didn't move till the car had pulled away.

As soon as I saw the taillights off in the distance, I walked back behind the counter to put my knife away hoping "Professor" Francisco never saw it. Too late.

"Cahrrrmeng, el cuchillo por favor." *The knife please.* He had his hand out, cigarette still in his lip.

"No."

"Is that your answer to everything, fighting?"

"I…I…I…it was three against one. W…w…w…what did you expect me to do?"

"En Español, por favor."

"NO! I don't care about Spanish! I don't care! Leave me alone!"

He started cleaning up the aisle, quietly picking up things off the floor. I went in the back and got the broom, mop, and some towels. When I returned to the front of the store, he had just come in from outside, flicking his cigarette out onto the curb. I felt bad. He had helped me. And he was a Professor, after all. And he owned the damn store. I had just yelled at a Professor and now my boss. Great.

"I'm sorry I yelled." I swept the floor and then added, "And thank you."

"You're welcome, Cahrrmeng." A few seconds later, "Give me the knife."

"Even if I were to give you the knife, I'd just get a new one. What do you think? I'm going to live in this town and not being able to defend myself? You don't get it. This is Boston, not Madrid. This is America."

"This is not America, Cahrrmeng." I hated his accent now. It was as if he was about to spit in the middle syllable of my name. "This is just Jamaica Plain. It's the small world you know."

"What?"

"This. This that you see…this is not America. This is just the little world you live in."

"I…I…I…I know," I said under my breath.

"Then why do you need a knife?"

"Just because…because, it scares people. People leave me alone. I'm not gonna kill anyone with it. Just scare them if they bother me."

"You could use words."

"I…I…I…could. Uggh. See. I can't. That's stupid. I…I…I…can't anyways."

"It's not stupid. If you know what to say and show power in it, you can always outsmart just about anyone. And most times, you don't even have to raise your voice."

I started writing down everything that had broken or been destroyed by the rich blonde girls so I could tally everything up. A lot of stuff broke. I was wondering if I'd get blamed for it all and have to pay for it.

"Cahhrrmeng, you can stop stuttering. You just need confidence. You need to believe you're smarter than those girls." He started mopping the floor now.

"I'm tougher than those girls."

"Smarter."

"I'm street smart. But they're rich smart. They have everything. I have nothing."

"You're smarter than those girls, Cahhrmeng. You just don't realize it."

"Yeah right I am."

"No, I mean, you are far more intelligent than they are. The stuttering—that's just you thinking you're vulnerable. Didn't you notice that when you got mad, you didn't stutter at all? Because you had a plan and you were ready to initiate it. It was a bad plan, but a plan nonetheless."

I didn't say anything at all. I kept pretending to write out the list.

"Mira," he said. *Look.* "I'll make a deal with you. If you promise to read, I'll pay you."

"What?"

"For every book you read I'll pay you…let's say…one dollar. Every Spanish book you read, two dollars."

"That's stupid."

"No. If you read more, you'll get rid of the stuttering. What do you have to lose? And you can make money doing it. What do you say?"

I hesitated. I was thinking about the extra cash. "I don't have time to read. I'm a slow reader. Plus, what are you getting out of it? Are you going to make me write a report or something? I have enough homework. I just want to dance. That's all I want to do. Why can't I just do that? I just want to go home. Nobody gets it."

He walked over to the door and picked up a piece of glass we'd missed. He walked back towards the counter and almost in a whisper he said, "You don't have to write a report. I won't test you on anything. It's the honor system. You can read while you're here working when you're done with your homework. You can read on the bus to school or on the trolley to practice. You can read before you go to bed. You can do it. And for every book you read, I'll pay you. And you'll see, the stuttering will go away, and…well, you'll just have to trust me."

I was tired. I didn't want to fight anymore. And I didn't want to start crying in front of this professor but for some reason, it's all I wanted to do. Cry. I changed the subject. "You're a big-time professor, huh? A…a…a…a…t Boston College or somewhere fancy like that? A place they'd never let someone like me in?"

"Yes. I'm a professor. But not at any college that wouldn't let you in." He smiled.

I gave in just to stop talking about it. "Okay. What book do I have to read? And where do I get it?"

"You can read any book you want. Your choice. And the library is a good start."

"Okay then."

"Good."

"Wait. *Professor* Francisco!"

He laughed. "Yes, Cahhrmeng?"

"I didn't see you come in the store. And you always come in when I'm here. That can't be right. Who are you? Wait. Al. I mean, Mr. McAdams has you check on me when he can't. And you're both teachers…and you really do own this place? Wow. I'm losing my touch. I should have picked up on that."

"Bravisimo." He smiled as he clapped his hands.

I had never been alone. All the nights I thought I was working by myself, he had been watching me. He lived right around the corner. A stone's throw away, I'd find out soon enough.

I first read books that were thin and easy to read. I was a slow reader, so I would even pick books way below my level of reading but he didn't care. I would come into the store and every week I'd show him a list of what I'd said I'd read. At first I mostly read books based on how many pages they were. And, although I tried to read some Spanish books, they really were out of my league, so the kid versions were the best. Sometimes I started a book and then didn't finish it, but told him I did. But he never asked me, never questioned anything, and always paid me no matter what.

But one day the librarian gave me a book, *The Hobbit*, by J.R.R. Tolkien. From the first page onward I was fascinated and engrossed. And when I went to work that following week I didn't want to just get paid; I started talking about the book with Professor Francisco. He didn't say a word, but stood there on the other side of the counter, listening. Even in my excitement back then I knew he was mighty proud of himself. Oh, it didn't stop my stuttering at all. That would come later, with a speech therapist, much later in my life. But it was the hook. And it worked.

One of the last times I saw Professor Francisco, he handed me a gift. It was a copy of the book, *The Prophet*, by Kahlil Gibran. He told me that I had earned it. And that he expected me to continue reading no matter what. And I told him that I would. That I loved to read and I thanked him for the book.

When I went to bed that night, comfortable on the couch, with the lights down low and the little flashlight in my hand, I opened to the first pages. Five crisp twenty-dollar bills with a little note fell out of the book. I gathered all the money up and read the note written in Spanish: "You must read at least one-hundred-dollars worth of books now. Remember, one dollar for English and two dollars for Spanish. F."

That was the best job I ever had.

***

I think if I had known you, and you were in my life, you would have paid me an allowance if we could have afforded it. When I dream, I dream big. That's how Mama taught me. And we'd be rich because you were some big, important man doing big, important things. And I would've read all those books anyway because you and I would've read them together, you know, on the weekends when you weren't working.

And the knife? I wouldn't have needed protection if you were around…

Mason

Mr. McAdams was a genius in many ways. Not only was he the best teacher I ever had, but the most caring one as well. AA was a constant for me, as well as school and performing. Although Mr. McAdams wasn't always sure of where I was or what I was doing, he could always count on me showing up for those three things without fail. It was made clear to me early on that unless I went to school I couldn't perform. And even though both of these institutions had nothing to do with each other, if I missed school, I'd be out of rehearsals and any competitions. I always had a feeling all of that was Mr. McAdams's doing.

AA started out as just somewhere for me to go when I needed a place to hang. But it also became a place where I found comfort in knowing that things were never as bad as I thought. And I learned so much. I'd try to "live one day at a time." I'd recite the Serenity Prayer when I got lost: "God, grant me the serenity to accept the things I cannot change, courage to change the things I can, and the wisdom to know the difference." I'd pride myself on trying every day to "Let go and let God," another AA "ism" that everyone said on a regular basis. In a lot of ways AA was my church, maybe more my therapy, especially in my teen years.

And then one day Mr. Mac, as everyone called Mr. McAdams for short, asked if I wanted to take a ride with him. I had no idea where we were going, but I jumped in the car and went along anyway. We had been talking about nothing in particular for quite some time when I noticed a sign: Massachusetts Correctional Institution.

"Um, where are we going?"

"You'll see soon enough," he said.

"Seriously, where are we going?" I was concerned.

After passing a mountain of trees, he pointed. "We're going in there. I want you to meet someone."

I waited a bit, hoping to see a shopping mall or something, but no. It was the prison.

I leaned all the way back into my seat. I was so mad. "What is this? A Scared Straight seminar or something? What the fuck? What the hell am I doing so wrong that everyone thinks I need help? Aren't I doing everything right? Why are you doing this to me?"

"Hey! Calm down! And watch your language," he yelled right back at me.

I was huffing and breathing heavily. I didn't want to go "meet" anyone. I'd seen enough people who were in and out of jail in my neighborhood my whole life and I never visited them. What the hell? I couldn't believe it.

He pulled into the parking lot gates. After getting a clearance, he then pulled into a parking spot and turned off the engine. I was just staring at the dashboard. I felt tricked and betrayed. My chest hurt. We sat there for minute.

"Carmen. Has it ever even dawned on you for one minute that maybe, just maybe, I'm bringing you here *not* because you need help, but maybe because I think you might be able to help someone else?"

I slowly looked over at Mr. Mac. I was still breathing deeply but had calmed down a bit. "Why? Why wouldn't you ask me first? And what could I possibly do to help someone in fucking prison?"

"Hey, enough with the language. Now, I did ask you— if you wanted to go for a ride. You didn't ask where, but I didn't force you into the car."

"Oh, come on, Mr. Mac! That's a trick and you know it."

"Nope. Sorry. You could have asked. We could have had this whole conversation back in Boston." Mr. Mac smiled and winked at me. I couldn't help it. He was right. I didn't ask.

"I'm just gonna say, for the record, I owe you one and Imma get you back. Now what am I doing here?" I tried to be fierce, but it came out a bit jokingly.

"We're going in to see a really good friend of mine, Mason. He's been in here for about a year now. He has a lot more time to serve, but I thought he wouldn't mind meeting someone I always talk about when I come and visit. He's in AA too."

Now it made a lot more sense to me. "Oh. What'd he do? You know, to get himself in here?"

"I think you should ask him that yourself. Okay? Ready to go?"

We made our way over to the facility and, after a few security checks, we were allowed to meet with Mason.

I was surprised. When he walked into the meeting room I had expected to see a Black man, a former gang member, or someone from the neighborhood. But Mason walked in the door with the blondest hair I'd ever seen—it was almost white—and the prettiest blue eyes. Besides the tattoos on his arms, he could've easily been the older brother of one of the rich kids I danced with from West Roxbury. He called Mr. Mac by his first name, Al, and they shook hands and did that manly hug thing.

Mr. Mac introduced us and we sat at the table while they caught up on things. And then Mr. Mac excused himself and said he had to do some paperwork to leave some money for Mason and that'd he'd be right back—conveniently leaving me and Mason alone to talk for a bit. I didn't know what to say, but Mason had no problem taking the lead.

"So, kid. Al tells me that you have no parents. True?"

"Yeah."

"And you carry?"

I was surprised Mr. Mac knew that, though clearly Francisco would have told him. "Yup."

"Just a knife or you gotta gun too?"

"W...w...w...why are you interrogating me? I'm not the one in prison," I said with an attitude.

He leaned back in his chair. "Fair. You're right. Sorry."

An uncomfortable moment passed. I wasn't expecting him to back down or apologize. I'd seen enough of those Scared Straight episodes to know the minute you mouthed off, they were in your face. And then I asked, "So, why you in here?"

He waited a moment and then leaned forward again, putting his hands on the table. "I carried. A knife. Two actually. I was a drunk and I liked to burglarize people's homes, and one night I kinda made use of the knife I thought I was just carrying to scare folk. I'm a drunk. I didn't mean to do it and I didn't know I…well, you get the picture."

"You murdered someone?" I couldn't believe I was sitting at a table so casually talking to a murderer.

"God no! Jesus, Mary and Joseph, keep your voice down!" he said, almost beside himself. "But, I hurt them bad enough. I didn't mean to. And if I hadn't been carrying…well, who knows, right?"

"Yeah," I said, almost under my breath, feeling sorry for him. "I'm not a drunk, you know," I added.

"I know, kid. But you don't need to put yourself in a situation that could land you here. From what I understand, you've got a pretty bright future ahead of you. It's what I hear anyways." He smiled and just then a bell rang. Our time was up.

Mr. Mac couldn't come back in once he left. He'd done that on purpose, of course. I said goodbye to Mason and he shook my hand and smiled as he headed on back to his cell. I walked on out to the lobby and met Mr. Mac there.

"So, how'd it go? Mason's a good guy, huh?" he said hopefully.

"Yeah. I feel bad for him. He seems nice enough. How long's he got?"

"Well, you don't need to feel bad for him. Pray for him all you want, but don't feel bad for him. He was given just as many chances as anyone else and he chose not to take them. And now he's taking responsibility for his actions and dealing with the consequences. He'll be fine. As long as he doesn't drink, he'll be fine. He's still got a few more years."

"Wow. Not sure how I helped him at all. I still think you wanted him to just tell me stuff to help me." I didn't want Mr. Mac to think I didn't know what he did.

"Nope, Ms. Carmen, you're wrong. Mason needed to share his story with someone who might hear it and change their ways because of it. It gives him purpose. It gives him hope. And besides loving someone, hope might be the best gift you give someone. Got it?"

"Got it."

I didn't stop carrying that day, but I did keep in touch with Mason over the following year through letters and through Mac. Mason wasn't much of a letter writer, but every now and then I'd receive a quick note thanking me for my letters and saying it was nice to hear about what was going on in the real world "on the outside." He'd always sign it with a big smiley face and just the letter "M."

The funny thing was, when I did stop carrying, it wasn't a conscious decision or anything like that. I don't even remember it. There wasn't some light bulb moment that made me throw it away or any one particular day where I just decided to stop carrying my knife. I just didn't need it anymore. So I stopped carrying.

* * *

Things always seemed to fall into place for me. Something I just can't explain but for all the things that I didn't have in my life, I seemed to always have exactly enough, certainly whatever I needed. And as unconventional as it may have seemed at the time, I always felt like people cared for me and loved me. Maybe it wasn't the court-appointed guardians who were "supposed to" love and take care of me, but whether it was Mason, Mr. Mac, Jackson, Francisco, or so many others in my life, I always felt an abundance of love. No matter where I went, people cared about me and I knew it...even if I didn't always appreciate it at first.

I never understood all those people that would go on talk shows and proclaim not knowing who they were because they never had a father. Usually they'd show these young girls on the Sally Jessy Raphael show and they'd be devastated and confused by how their lives had turned out. I was always intrigued by that. Somehow they believed that if they had just known who their father was, they would have been better off. They'd talk about not knowing who they were because they didn't understand where they came from. They'd talk about how they missed not having a father. And then Sally or Phil Donahue would bring out the long-lost dad and there'd be cries and smiles and joy.

And I'd sit there numb and so confused. How can you miss something you never had?

Lowell

I first met the twins, Michelle and Julia Lowell, when I was in the third grade. We had just moved into the neighborhood and I started going to the same Catholic school, Blessed Sacrament. It was a very working class and blue collar kind of neighborhood, and most of the kids—if they even went to school—generally went to different public schools all over the city. But not me. Mama wasn't going to let me go to any public school and however she did it, she got me into that expensive Catholic school.

Of course, we were one of the poorest families. But, pride was important to Mama and it rubbed off on me too. I'd rather pretend I was fine than let anyone know that I wasn't okay. And I was so good at it that most times people believed what I told them.

Now, the Lowell girls were rich compared to everyone else in school. Of course they were White, but they also had a house across the street from the school, and if you were their friend they would invite you to their pool parties! They had both their parents living at home (which was a rarity in our neighborhood), the nicest clothes, and they were clearly the most popular girls in school.

In the third grade, when other kids were making fun of this little girl named Roberta, who was really slow and wore glasses and definitely had some developmental issues, it was the cool Lowell girls who intervened and stopped it. That's when I knew I wanted to be friends with them. They were popular for all the right reasons.

I think it was Michelle who first befriended me in grammar school. It started because day after day I would sit alone at lunch drinking the free milk I got from the school program. And it wasn't that Mama didn't send me with money to buy lunch, or some days have a sandwich for me; it was just that sometimes I'd use the money in the morning to buy a soda or M&M's for breakfast. It was never enough money to buy lunch in the school cafeteria anyway, and, well, most days I just didn't show up with lunch.

But for Michelle, it just seemed wrong. And so one day she sat next to me and simply pushed half her sandwich, still in the plastic wrap, over my way. Under her breath, almost sternly, but not even looking at me she said, "I don't want it. So go on, eat it."

That's how Michelle was. She was a pretty tough girl. One of the reasons she was popular was because you knew she could kick anyone's ass at any time. She was fiercely athletic, really pretty, and she was smarter than most everyone in the class, easily. When Michelle told me to eat that sandwich, I didn't dare say anything different. I just sat there and ate it happily and quietly.

Julia was different. She was, of course, just as pretty as Michelle because they were twins, after all, but she was the sweet one. She was kindhearted and always the one explaining things completely. Michelle might have said, "Eat it," and Julia would then come by and explain that they had had a huge breakfast and that's why Michelle and her weren't that hungry—oh, and by the way, here's a bag chips and some cookies that she couldn't eat either because she was just too full. And somehow, I'd end up with a better lunch than they did.

After Mama died, Michelle and Julia just started bringing me a bag lunch every day. It wasn't discussed; it just was what they did. At some point, Julia mentioned that her mother just said to bring me a lunch and that I was always welcome if I needed a place to stay. And one day, way after the third grade, the day after Charlie died, to be exact, I showed up at their doorstep.

I remember when Mr. Lowell opened the door. I was dirty, tired, and had rehearsed the whole way on the bus what I was going to say. And before I could open my mouth, Mr. Lowell just said, "Well, it took you long enough. The girls are upstairs. Dinner will be ready in a bit. Barbeque out on the patio. Go on."

Mr. Lowell was a towering figure. He would have been scary if he didn't have that sweet disposition about him. He was kind from the bottom of his heart and the minute he spoke, you just felt it. In fact, I would say he was lovely. He was exactly what I thought a dad should be like. He was balding just a bit, wore glasses, and always came back home with a story from work. He then would put the Red Sox game on TV and ask his family how they were. He truly couldn't have been more of a perfect dad if I had made him up.

Mrs. Lowell was coming down the stairs and saw me standing in the hall by the door. She had short brown hair and a smile that could knock you over from across the room. In a lot of ways, she reminded me of my own mother. She was a mother-shaped mother, not too big, not too small, and she was so beautiful. That's where the girls got it from. She had that twinkle in her eye, the same one Mama had. Clearly, she had heard Mr. Lowell say a few words to me but thought he was talking to her upstairs. When she made it down the staircase and saw me it seemed to all click. She came right over to me and hugged me. Cupping my face in her hands, she said, "Everything's gonna be just fine." And I nodded. In the next breath she yelled up to Julia and Michelle that I was home.

Over the next years, I would stay with the Lowells at various times. I would sleep on the couch downstairs whenever I did stay over, and, even though I was treated like part of the family by having chores to do and responsibilities, I was never forced to stay or do anything at all. I could come and go as I pleased. Although I'd always give a reason that I was staying at someone else's house or that I was going to rehearsal, it was never required. I think the Lowells just always wanted me to know that, no matter what I did, there would be a home for me to go to. And more times than not, even when I lost my way, they'd be right there with their door open allowing me once again to stay on the couch.

And I did lose my way. More than once.

I had fallen in love.

Well, that's what I thought it was—love, anyways.

I had met a guy named Geraldo. He worked for his dad who owned a security company, so he always carried a gun. Talk about rich, his family was thick in it. Geraldo wasn't that good looking, but he worked out a lot, had a great body, and always bought me things. New shoes, new clothes, new jewelry—anything I wanted. And being that I was quite humble and grateful for anything at all, he thought I was unlike any other girl he knew.

He also drove this very cool Camaro. It was souped-up with the best, most expensive parts money could buy. Everyone knew his car. You knew he was on his way before he even showed up because the engine was so loud. I loved that. And he was always coming to see me.

I met Geraldo when I worked as a bagger at a local supermarket. His father's company provided an armed security guard for the store and, at times, Geraldo would work the store when the regular security guard couldn't.

Later on I'd find out he was working more days just to see me.

At first, things were perfect. He'd take me out to nice restaurants, but only after taking me shopping to buy a new outfit or a new pair shoes. I never had to take the bus or walk anywhere—wherever I needed to go, Geraldo was there to take me. I was in heaven. He'd take me to rehearsal, take me to school, pick me up from school. I was almost seventeen and in eleventh grade when we met. For the first time in my life, I knew what I wanted—I wanted someone to love me this much.

And then, things changed. I can't say I noticed it outright at first, not even later on when I should have, when even my friends were pointing it out. He convinced me that I didn't need to go to work. Then, of course, it crept into not needing to be around my friends, not needing to go to rehearsals, and, eventually, that I didn't even need to go to school.

I started to feel shut in. Claustrophobic. And finally, one day I told him. He was so angry with me. He told me that I didn't care for him and that I didn't truly understand what it was to love someone. He started bringing up the idea that if I would just give myself to him, if I would let him be my first, then he would believe me and trust me. I wasn't ready for that just yet. I didn't want to sleep with him or anyone. I was still a virgin. But I knew if I didn't do something he would leave me. We compromised. If he'd let me go to school, I'd be naked every night and he could touch me, but he'd have to promise nothing else. He agreed, but only if he could drop me off and pick me up from school. And I agreed.

But that was worse.

As soon as the bell rang for lunch we'd all hang outside, eat sandwiches, smoke cigarettes, and talk. Out of nowhere you'd hear Geraldo's car blare up the street. He'd park on the sidewalk and make me talk to him the whole time. When it was time to leave school, I'd be walking my friends to the bus stop, making plans to maybe get together later, and he'd pull up and pressure me to get in the car quickly. This started happening all the time, every single day, and things were just getting scary.

One night, at his father's house, he threw me on the bed. At first I thought he was playing around, but he then took out his gun and started gliding it along the side of my body. He started at my ankles and then slowly went up the side of my legs. I hated guns. I was afraid of guns and he knew it. I stopped smiling and laughing and asked him to stop. And he just laughed. He put the gun to my stomach and started kissing me, cocking and uncocking the gun. I knew it was a Beretta. He talked about it all the time, and I'd seen it more than once because he wore it in a holster like a cop. He also had one on his ankle. Ironically, it was another part of him that at first intrigued me—not the danger part—but that he was using guns to protect people, instead of harming them. Or so I thought.

I was petrified. The gun for sure, but I knew there was no way of getting out of having sex with him. I was so scared. And he found my fear tantalizing. I begged him to please put the gun away, to please stop pushing me, and he got more energized. His father, a clearly disgusting man, was asking him through the door in Spanish if he'd finished yet. Had he made me a real woman yet? His father knew. He was in on it. His father had pushed him to have sex with me. Geraldo wasn't even paying attention to me now. He was going to do this whether I wanted him to or not.

With the gun in his hand laying against my temple, he continued undressing me as I cried. He told me that all girls always cry the first time, and that I'd be happy that he forced me once he was done. I stopped trying to stop him.

The amount of pain feeling him thrust himself upon me was excruciating. I kept trying to push him off of me, but he held both my hands with one of his, while he held the gun with the other. I could see the shiny barrel out of the corner of my eye, and I just kept looking at it till he finished.

When he was done, he got off of me and put on his pants and went into the other room with his father. I could hear him laughing and slapping hands with his father, telling him that he had "finished the job." I got up off the bed; I was bleeding and in so much pain. I went into the bathroom and when I got there, I threw up. I saw myself in the mirror and realized that I had let someone hurt me. Maybe I deserved it. Maybe I put myself in the position and deserved exactly what I got. What did I think was going to happen when I got fancy clothes, new shoes, and went out to eat? Of course I was going to have to pay for it somehow. And I cried. I sat on the floor half-naked and cried. Geraldo never even noticed.

The next day he drove me to school and I was ashamed of myself. He kissed me and behaved as if nothing had happened. As if we had somehow become closer. He never asked if I was okay. He never cared. And I knew he never would.

That day in school, Julia noticed that I was not feeling well. I didn't want to tell her so I tried to pretend I was okay. But she knew. And she told me as sweetly and kindly as possible that whatever it was, she'd be there for me no matter what. I smiled and walked away.

Later that day in the girls' bathroom as I was throwing up again, Julia followed me in and demanded that I tell her what was wrong. Michelle followed her in right afterwards. I didn't say anything because I was so embarrassed, but Michelle just guessed it. They knew he was treating me badly and that I couldn't get away. But having them both there telling me they'd be there for me was what I needed to hear, even if I didn't truly believe there was anything they could do for me. I'd made my bed, and now I'd have to deal with the consequences.

The following weekend was the prom. I had a lovely white dress with beautiful white shoes and was so excited to finally be able to see all of my friends somewhere other than in school. Geraldo had agreed to go only to shut me up and get me in bed again. I had told him—and it was true—that I was so sore and still bleeding that I couldn't have sex with him unless he wanted to deal with all the blood. That was enough to curl his stomach. I don't think I was ever so grateful to have my period in all my life, but that week I was thankful beyond belief. The whole time I was trying to think of ways to get away from this situation, but it was getting harder to believe I'd be able to.

Of course, we didn't get to the prom on time. Instead, we got there about two hours late, and after being there a very short time we got into another fight. He told me we were leaving, and even though I didn't want to go, I didn't really have much choice. I didn't get to say goodbye to everyone, but I did manage to let Julia know I was leaving.

As we made our way to the elevator, the door opened and I was surprised to see an old friend I hadn't seen since grammar school. Kevin. He was the first boy I ever kissed. I think I was eleven years old at the time. He was getting off the elevator with Claire, one of the girls in our class who didn't hang out with us very much, but they were clearly dating. I didn't recognize him at first, and he didn't recognize me either, but as he stepped out of the elevator it dawned on both of us who the other was. I smiled at him, he said my name, "Hey, Carmen!" and the doors closed.

I was smiling. I thought he looked so handsome and it had been a long time. I was about to share with Geraldo who Kevin was, but he was already fuming. He'd been fuming and angry all night. But now he was sure I was cheating on him. "Who the fuck was that? Your boyfriend? Is that why you don't want to have sex with me? You'd rather fuck that stupid-ass White boy?"

"What?" I said shocked. "Kevin was my boyfriend in sixth grade."

"Oh, that's your old fucking boyfriend, huh? I bet you gave him a piece and you're just holding out on me. You fucking whore." He was pissed. And I remembered he was still carrying his gun. "Get the fuck in the car."

I knew if I got in the car, I'd have to sleep with him and worse, he'd hurt me. I hadn't seen him this angry so I knew it was bad. I didn't know what to do. And before I could think, he opened the car door and shoved me in.

As we drove out of the parking lot, he peeled around the corner and sped through the other cars. I was screaming for him to slow down and all he kept saying was that I was a whore and that he was going to teach me what a real man was.

As he reached the on-ramp, it got real quiet. There were no cars on the freeway but he finally slowed down just a bit. He was still mumbling terrible things under his breath but I kept thinking about how empty the streets were. I knew I had made a mistake by leaving the party and getting in that car.

Geraldo then looked over at me and asked me what I was thinking about. I didn't hear him and he yelled at me again. I looked at him briefly, but I didn't say a word. He yelled at me to say something. I didn't move. I kept staring out the window, trying to figure out how I would leave his house in the middle of the night without tripping the alarm. And then, he started yelling again. Asking me if I was thinking about my boyfriend, Kevin, and if I wished I was back there with him. That maybe I was really a queer and wanted to be with a girl instead. He was crazed.

I looked over at him, confused as to how ridiculous he sounded, and out of nowhere he slugged me, full closed fist. The hit was so hard my head swung back to the chair and blood exploded out of my nose and into my mouth. My white dress was covered in red and I could feel my face blowing up. Without even thinking, I grasped the car door handle and jumped out of the car. I hit the freeway pavement hard and then rolled, and rolled, and rolled onto the damp, muddy ground. I heard the car squealing to a halt. I couldn't move. There was dirt and blood in my mouth. I knew I had to get up or he would come and kill me, and no one would be the wiser. I was more afraid than I'd ever been. But I was in so much pain.

And as I lay there, I heard him walking towards me. I was sure this was it. Maybe he wouldn't kill me. Maybe he'd feel sorry for me and maybe he'd be nice since I was so hurt. And then I heard it…

"Carmen? Carmen, where are you? Are you okay?" It was Julia.

"I'm here. I'm here," I tried to say loudly.

And all of a sudden, there was Julia, kneeling by my side, wiping my face with her sweater. Michelle was at my legs, trying to take the leaves and branches off of me. They brought other classmates with them. Tyler picked me up and carried me to the car. Michelle made mention that Kevin noticed something was wrong. Julia had known all along that something was wrong and had never let me out of her sight. So the whole time while we were at the party, Geraldo and I were being watched. The minute they saw me get into the car and leave the prom, a bunch of them decided to follow us just in case. Thankfully they did.

I was driven to Michelle and Julia's house and carried into the living room. Mr. and Mrs. Lowell had been waiting up, thinking that the girls would be home much later. When we walked in the door, Mrs. Lowell ordered Pauline, their older sister, to run upstairs and get some towels and a first aid kit. Michelle ran into the kitchen to get me some water and I drank it as if I hadn't had water in days.

Mr. Lowell asked what happened and I was so embarrassed I couldn't say anything at all. Julia and Michelle pieced the whole story together, the whole time looking at me kindly, hoping that I'd understand telling their parents the entire story was the right thing to do.

There was talk of taking me to the hospital, but I refused. I was okay. So Mrs. Lowell then ordered me into a bathroom so she could clean me up good. And without saying a word, she cleaned my wounds and bandaged me. She was angry, disappointed. I couldn't look at her. I was embarrassed. She said, "You're staying here for the next few weeks. Understood?"

"Yes, Ma'am."

She walked out into the living room and I looked at myself in the mirror. What had I done?

I walked out slowly from the bathroom. I could hear the discussion going on in the living room. "Does she need to go to the hospital?" Mr. Lowell was asking.

"No, honey, she's fine. Some scratches and bruises. The real damage is on the inside. Girls, go upstairs to bed please. We'll talk about this more tomorrow."

I could hear Michelle, Julia, and Pauline run up the stairs. My bed was the living room couch, so I was sure the coast was clear and I could go sit and be alone. When I walked into the living room, sitting in his chair was Donald, Mr. Lowell. He was smoking a cigarette.

I had my head down. I was so humiliated. I was fluffing the pillow on the sofa and he got up from his chair and sat down on the couch.

"Sit down. Right here," he said.

I sat down next to Mr. Lowell, still with my head down. He put his arm around me.

"You okay?"

I looked up slowly. "Yes. Thank you. Thank you for taking me in again."

He put out his cigarette in the ash tray. "You know you're welcome here any time."

"I know."

There was an awkward silence. And Mr. Lowell stood up. "So, this guy. Enough okay? We'll get a restraining order if we have to."

"Oh, uhem…I…I…I…"

"You thought that was a question." He sat back down. "Carmen, no one deserves to be hit. And, as long as I'm alive, no one is going to hit one of mine."

I kept looking down. Feeling so horrible. So scared. "He has a gun," I whispered.

"Good. It'll be a fair fight." He winked. I started crying again and he hugged me. "Do you know why I call you 'Plan B'?"

I laughed a little through my tears and answered, "No, not really."

"Well, because, if those three girls of mine don't work out, you're next on deck." We both laughed. He kissed me on the head and then talked seriously. "No one feels sorry for you Carmen. You've had it tough, but you're a tough kid. You're a good kid. You deserve better. No one who truly loves you would hit you. No one who truly knows who you really are would ever hit you. And a real man would never hit a girl. I never want to hear that someone hit you ever again. Got it?"

"Yes."

"Okay, go to bed."

"Good night, Mr. Lowell." I snuggled under the covers as he walked on over to the doorway.

When he got to the light he turned around. "Tomorrow, we'll get a restraining order. Maybe I'll have a talk with that boy first, but you're done with him."

"I know."

"Okay then. Good night, Plan B." And he turned off the light.

The next morning, I woke when Julia came down the stairs. My eye had turned black and blue, my lip was fat, and the bruises on my sides were hurting. I could hardly move. Julia had gotten me new dressings and a change of clothing. Michelle was in the kitchen helping Mrs. Lowell make breakfast. It was Sunday, and I should have already been up, but I had finally cried myself to sleep early in the morning, and they let me sleep.

As Julia stepped closer to help me change, we heard the roar of the Camaro outside. It was loud and clearly right in front of the house. Geraldo kept revving the engine louder. I started to get up, thinking I would talk to him and tell him to leave. Julia pushed me down, though it didn't take much at all, I was in so much pain. "Dad's taking care of this, Carmen. You stay right here."

Michelle, Pauline, and Mrs. Lowell walked into the living room and we all looked out the same window. We had a clear view of what was about to go down. Mr. Lowell walked out onto his porch, and four other neighbors, guy neighbors from next door, came out the house as well. Two of them were holding bats. They stood on either side of Mr. Lowell as he walked closer to the car. Geraldo got out.

"I'm here to get Carmen," Geraldo said.

"No you're not, son," Mr. Lowell said. "And I suspect you won't be bothering her ever again."

"Whatt'ya talking about? She's mine. I'll bother her whenever I goddamn want."

Mr. Lowell seemed even taller than his six feet now. He towered over Geraldo, and all of the neighbors made Geraldo look real small. What a loser.

"Let me put it this way, son. If you ever touch one of my daughters ever again, I'll kill you myself. Understood?"

"She's not your daughter."

"Son, you sure you want to argue that point with me? Let me put it this way: you touch any of my girls, including Carmen, I'll kill you myself. Is that easier for you to understand?" He flicked his cigarette almost all the way across the street.

Geraldo didn't say a word. He seemed to contemplate what to say. One of the neighbors holding a bat, Mr. O'Brien, added, "And don't bring that car around here anymore. It's too loud. If I see it around here again, I'll burn the fucking thing."

Geraldo looked over our way into the window. I didn't move. I wasn't afraid. I felt empowered. I didn't even really know the neighbors, but they stood next to Mr. Lowell because that's what neighbors do. And here I was, in this home, loved. Cared for. Treated like one of the family. What did I have to be afraid of? Nothing.

That was the first and last time a man ever hit me.

I never saw or heard from Geraldo again.

* * *

People would ask me all the time what it was like to grow up without parents. And I'd always answer that it was fine. That it had its ups and downs, like any other childhood, I suppose, but they'd never believe me.

They'd continue on and ask, "But what happened to your parents?" And I'd tell them about Mama and they'd make that sad face as if they wished they could have done something for me had they only had a magic wand or something. And I'd think they'd be done with the mini-interrogation and I'd be wrong, of course. They'd want to know about you. "What happened to your father?"

It was just easier to tell everyone you died when Mama was six months pregnant with me. It explained why I knew nothing about you and made Mama look better than trying to explain her mistake—of keeping such a secret and thinking she'd live a lot longer than she would.

At some point, I started just answering the question this way: "I grew up with a lot of different families, with a lot of different parents."

That was a good thing.

The Watsons

I'll never forget the day I learned I wasn't a "real" Black girl. I remember it like it was yesterday.

My mother had this friend, named Mrs. Watson. And Mrs. Watson and her family lived in Roxbury, Massachusetts. Sometimes on the weekend my mom and I would take the bus on over to visit the Watsons. They had two girls and two boys. Rhea, the youngest, was exactly the same age as me and, naturally, my best friend.

See, the Watsons were rich. Mrs. Watson had this beautiful home. It had lots of rooms. Bedrooms for each of the kids, a living room with a baby grand piano, a family room where the TV was—and they even had two fireplaces. Our little apartment we lived in then could fit in their kitchen. They also had a huge backyard with grass where they would have barbeques and the neighborhood would come over and eat hot dogs and hamburgers along with all the fixings: creamy potato salad, macaroni and cheese, fried chicken, sweet potato pie…mmmm. The works! And you could drink as much soda as you wanted. I always wondered if Mama thought this was her dream home too.

Even though we were just visiting, we always had to go to church. Their church. Mrs. Watson's church was a very different church than the boring sleep-inducing Catholic church I had to go to for school. For one, churchgoing with the Watson's was an all-day event! We'd wake up in the morning, get dressed, pack up all the food Mrs. Watson had cooked all night, and we would make our way over to church at the crack of dawn. When we got there, we'd have to get re-dressed into our "church outfits," which were never what I was wearing, but a borrowed dress or gown from my best friend, Rhea. I always remember thinking I didn't even have ONE of these dresses for a special occasion. Rhea had many—enough to share. I don't think I ever wore the same Sunday dress twice!

I don't remember exactly what church denomination it was, but it wasn't boring Catholic church, that's for sure. It was colorful. Women were dressed in their best outfits and the biggest hats you'd ever seen. The men were also outdoing each other with fancy, pinstriped, double-breasted suits. Sometimes, especially on the holidays, you'd easily see two or three men wearing a purple or green colored suit. Amazing.

And the music—I don't think the preacher ever spoke. Everything seemed to have a rhythm to it. The choir sang the whole time. The preacher would speak a sentence, the choir would chime in with a chorus, almost like backing him up. And you couldn't help but get all caught up in it. People would be dancing in the aisles, singing and "praising Him." It was like a full day of joy being at that Church.

And everybody seemed to love each other. When service was over, you'd hear people talking to each other as they made their way to where all the food was and calling each other "Sista' Mabel," or "Sista' Janet," or "Sista' this" or "Brotha' that." Everyone seemed so connected, so loving.

I always stayed close to Rhea, quietly observing.

After church I would go back home with the Watsons and help clean up and organize for dinner. Mama never came with us to church—at least, I don't remember her ever being there. Mama would leave me there and when Mrs. Watson would explain to other church folk who the "little addition" was, she would always say, "Her Mama's working. Doing the Lord's work and more to put food on the table." And the church folk person would respond, "Thank you Jesus." And Mrs. Watson would continue on, "Yes. Amen. We're blessed to be able to have Ms. Carmen with us today." And the church folk person, or, if there were two, would respond, almost in unison, "Hallelujah! Amen!"

I always felt so welcomed, even if I felt a little awkward. There was a sense of community that was different than in my neighborhood. It's not that it was better. But it was different. Maybe it was because these people had money? I don't know. But there was a comfort about being Black that was different than being Latina. And I liked being Black.

Or so I thought.

One weekend when I was dropped off at the Watsons' I said goodbye to Mama and went out to play with Rhea. We would walk the neighborhood, play across the street in the school parking lot, and just sit and talk. Rhea's sister, Wendy, was older. She was a teenager and, although we couldn't really hang with her, she was very protective of Rhea and, by default, me as well.

This particular day Mrs. Watson told Wendy that she needed to braid Rhea's hair for her because she wouldn't have time. So Wendy hurried us up and we headed on over to a her friend's house. And, there in the kitchen, set up like it was a doctor's office, were all these girls doing their hair. Combs were on the stove getting red hot, grease jars were lined up on the table along with thick combs, thin combs, brushes, beads, tiny elastics, sewing needles…there was so much stuff and eight girls doing each other's hair. Some of them were older than Wendy, but not by much. Maybe the oldest was twenty or something but, nonetheless, all of them were getting their hair done. Braided. Cornrowed. Something I had never done. My hair was always in pigtails or two braids. Mama never used grease in my hair. The most I got was a dab of V05 to calm down the frizz. Then my mom would brush my hair on the left side, put it in an elastic, braid it, do the other side, and we were done. Ten minutes at most—and most of that was me hating having my hair done. Some nights, after getting my hair washed, I would sleep with rollers in my head so it would look straight the next day. And yet most days my hair ended up in pigtails anyways. It would just look less frizzy after using the rollers.

But this, this was a project. An art project. It looked as serious as surgery. But it was a normal way of doing things on this side of town. I sat in the corner, watching as the tiny little braids were being braided along Rhea's scalp and grease was applied. This took hours. They were laughing and talking about boys and just plain ol' gossiping. It was such a girl thing to do.

Wendy stayed for a while and then, when she noticed the time, she said to the other girls, "Imma head on out for a bit, you guys got me covered?" And there was a roar of laughter in the room. Michelle shouted out, without stopping or looking up from the head she was braiding, "Girl, you best get on over there or he's gonna dump you big time and find someone else." And all the girls laughed. I just looked at Rhea, who also seemed confused. Wendy turned to me and then on over to Rhea and said, "I'm running out for a bit. I'll be back. And if you guys don't tell Ma, I'll make sure to get you ice cream later, okay?" Rhea answered back, "Uh huh," as if she'd done this too many times with her sister. And I replied with my very manner-esque and proper, "Yes, Wendy."

When Wendy left, the other girls seemed to make a swarm for me. Michelle asked if I wanted to get my hair done too. I shrugged my shoulders and saw Rhea smile. I wanted so badly to have tiny little braids on the top of my head dangling down with pretty beads too. And so Michelle told me to take my hair out and brush it, while she finished up with her current "client."

When I sat in the chair, Michelle started touching my hair and, at first, it felt really good. "Tania, come over here. Touch this girl's hair." Tania, who was a big, fat, Black girl, came on over and got all in it. "Oh, girl, that's some good hair. She got some of that White-folk hair." And then there was a big, roaring laugh from everyone. A bit unsure of what was so funny, I pretended to laugh too. But as I looked at Rhea, who was still getting the second half of her hair done, I could tell this wasn't a good thing, and that maybe I should stop laughing.

"Marcy, you need to look at this girl's hair. Pretty, huh?" Tania beckoned. She looked through the parts of my hair like she was looking for lice.

"She needs a lot of grease, that's why she got that nasty frizz," Marcy chimed in. "That's easy hair to straighten. She just don't know how to take care of it. She probably got a White mama. Yo mama White, girl?" she asked me.

I shook my head no and Tania, with her big fat hand, smacked me upside the head real hard. "Don't move your head when I'm working on it. Stupid dumbass White girl."

"You know what her problem is, right?" squealed Michelle. "She thinks she's better cuz she got that dang-on good hair." They all laughed and mumbled other things. I stared at Rhea, who was across the way from me still getting her hair done. It was as if she was trying to tell me something by ESP and I heard it. "Be quiet. Don't say one word."

Michelle started lining my scalp with grease that was on the table. It was too much and the grease started slathering down the sides of my face and forehead. She pretended not to notice and started braiding my hair anyways. The tiny braids starting at my left temple and going over my ear were hurting me so bad I couldn't help but squint. By the time she got to start the second row of braiding next to that one, my eyes were tearing. Tania came back on over when she was done with her "client" and looked at my head. "What the hell is this girl crying for? What? You never had your head done?" My head was cocked over to the right; I didn't want to move and wasn't sure what to answer. As I was about to say something, she screamed at me, "I'm talking to you, honkey wannabe!"

Rhea screamed from the other side of the room, "Leave her alone!"

"Ah, this is your little White friend," Tania said. "You and your family think you're better than us with your big house and your cars. And now you have your little White friends. How quaint." They all laughed.

The grease kept running down my face and it was getting in my eyes. I was tearing up because the braids hurt so bad. Marcy made a point of saying over and over again that I was tender-headed, a word I'd never heard till then. "Ladies, you shouldn't even bother putting braids in that child's head. She ain't gonna make it. Look at her. Ya only on the fourth braid and that child's about to die. I'd put the hot comb to it and just straighten it out for her. That's probably what she's used to anyways. It'd probably look pretty too."

Tania agreed. Michelle started taking out the braids with the comb. She seemed to dig into my scalp even harder just to make the point that I was tender-headed. "Look at her, she can't even take a comb to her dumbass honkey head! Tender-headed little bitch."

The hot comb had been put on the stove to get ready to straighten my hair. I'd never had a hot comb put to my hair; I was just glad they had stopped trying to braid my hair. I was so afraid to move that I didn't say anything at all when the comb came off the stove red hot and steaming. Rhea was restless, as if she was watching a poor animal be abused. But she was confined to her chair too. All the braids were nearly done on her head, but she couldn't move either if she had tried.

Before Michelle put the comb through my hair she slapped me again and told me that I'd better stay still or this would burn that pretty White-like skin. I didn't move an inch.

The comb smoked as it went through the first part of my hair. The girls laughed at how much smoke was coming out. As Michelle pulled the comb through my hair it burned my scalp and burned my skin, and it took off all the hair that tangled in it. I screamed out loud, and jumped out of the chair from the burn. Rhea jumped on top of me as if to protect me. Even the "hairdressers" were stunned by what had happened. It was quiet except for my sobs underneath Rhea's little body.

Just then, Wendy walked right back in. "What the hell is going on here?"

No one said a word.

She took Rhea off of me.

My scalp, ear, and neck had been burned. The hair on the right hand side of my head had been burned off. It lay next to me, shriveled up and tinged. I had no hair above my right ear. It had burned right off.

"Oh my God! Oh my God! What the hell happened?" Wendy screamed.

Tania came over and said, "It's her fault. She's tender-headed and couldn't handle it but begged us to do her hair. She couldn't handle it so we were going to straighten it for her so she'd look all pretty and she moved and got all scared and that's how the comb got stuck in her head and burned her. Stupid little good-haired bitch. I told you not to move!"

Rhea, with all she could, screamed backed, "You are such a liar! You lie! Carmen didn't do anything at all. She didn't ask for anything at all. Wendy, I swear, she didn't do anything at all. They kept hitting her, they kept calling her honkey! They put too much grease in her hair. They burned her, Wendy."

"Go on in that icebox and get me some ice and some butter, Rhea." Wendy demanded. She walked over to me and lifted me up off the ground. She took a towel off the nearby table and gently started wiping away the grease that had dripped down my neck and forehead. She didn't touch my ear or the burnt part of my neck. "You safe now, baby girl, okay? I'm sorry I left you here."

The other girls stood there motionless. Wendy wrapped the ice in the towel and told me to hold it to my ear. She put butter on my neck. She then grabbed a fat elastic and gently wrapped the rest of my hair as best she could in a scarf and tied it all down with the fancy rubber band. She looked at Rhea and told her, "You and Carmen go home okay? Tell Mama what happened. You tell her everything. And tell her I'll be back shortly."

As soon as Rhea and I left through the doorway, you could hear Wendy yelling. It sounded as if furniture was being moved and someone was getting hit. I flinched a couple of times thinking we should go back and help, and Rhea looked at me again with the same fierce eyes she had when she sat across from me in the room. "No way."

When we walked into the house, Mr. and Mrs. Watson and both of Rhea's brothers were in the kitchen. The minute Mrs. Watson saw me she grabbed me away from Rhea and started looking at my wounds and my shredded hair. "Talk now and talk quickly, Rhea, what happened to this child?" she demanded. Rhea started telling the story, and when she was barely through the first half of it, the Watson boys had heard enough. They knew Wendy might be in danger and they jumped out of their chairs and headed on out the door.

Mrs. Watson gently unwrapped the headdress. I could tell by her face she was holding back a scream. Most of the hair on one side was clear off my head. My scalp and ear were charred and my neck was raw and covered in butter. She breathed in deeply and shook her head. I could feel her trying to hold back tears at the mess in front of her. She kept mumbling something about Jesus and forgiving her. "How you feel, sweetheart? You okay? Does it still burn? Do you have a headache, or do you feel sick? Tell me the truth, okay?" I looked quickly over at Rhea, who looked just as sad as her mother. I must have looked awful.

"No Ma'am, I feel just fine," I lied.

She smiled at me kindly. "Rhea, run down to your brother's room and get me a clean t-shirt for this girl to wear. She needs to put something on comfortable and roomy. Then get me a couple of face towels and two bath towels and bring them on in here."

"Yes, ma'am." Rhea ran downstairs to collect the t-shirt, then you could hear her in the hallway linen closet getting all the towels.

Mrs. Watson had put a bowl of soapy water on the table and a bowl of clear water. When Rhea returned she grabbed one of the face towels, put it in the soapy water, and started rubbing small sections of my hair gently to try and take out the enormous amount of grease. She didn't want to put me under the bath till "that wound scabbed over" so, for now, she'd need to do this by hand. She then alternated with the clean water, all the while singing a church tune, sometimes just humming, sometimes with the lyrics. There was something so soothing about it all.

As time passed and I was finally all cleaned up and changed into a t-shirt, Wendy and the boys returned. Mr. Watson was parking the car in the driveway. You could feel the aura in the room change. Wendy had a black eye and her hair was all over the place. Clearly, she had been in a fight, if not more.

Mrs. Watson ordered us to bed. Without a word, Rhea and I both turned and walked out of the kitchen. "I'll be there in a minute," Mrs. Watson mentioned, as we walked out the kitchen door.

Rhea's room was like it belonged to a few princesses. She had twin beds for when her friends would visit. Everything in the room was pink and white. I knew which bed was mine when I visited and I climbed right in. Rhea knelt before her bed to pray and, as I saw her do so, I got out of bed as well and knelt on my side, pretending I knew what I was doing.

When Rhea was done, I waited a few seconds more and then pretended I was done too. Mrs. Watson walked into the room. She walked over to Rhea and kissed her on the forehead goodnight and then walked over to my bed and sat next to me.

"You feeling a little better now, angel?" she said sweetly.

"Yes, ma'am."

"Well, tomorrow I'm gonna take you to the doctor's and then a fancy hairdressing place and see if we can't do something with your hair, okay?" she said in hopeful, almost sad voice.

"Okay. Thank you," I said sheepishly. "Ma'am?"

"Yes?"

I sat up in the bed. Rhea looked up as well. "Mrs. Watson, she saved me. She really did. Please don't…"

She cut me off. "She wouldn't have needed to save you, angel girl, if she hadn't put you and her little sister in harm's way. That's not saving someone, little lady. That's being irresponsible."

"But Mama—" Rhea tried to chime in, but was also cut off.

"Enough. Both of you to bed. This is no longer any of your business." She started tucking me in. "Everyone knows the rules in this house. You follow the rules or you choose not to, either way, there are consequences to both. Now, both of you, I expect you to be asleep by the time I walk out this bedroom door. Good night, girls."

She turned off the light as she walked out the door.

A few minutes passed and you could hear parts of the "conversation" going on in the kitchen almost perfectly.

"…what if that child had been burned worse? What if they did something to disfigure that child's face for life? How would you be feeling right now?" Mrs. Watson bellowed. "What exactly were you thinking? Huh? What were you thinking?"

"I wasn't, Mama. I'm so sorry," Wendy begged.

"Over a boy? You willing to risk a child's life over a boy? I raised you better than that young lady. I raised you better than that!"

"I know, Mama. I know. I'm so sorry." Wendy's cries were heartfelt.

"Don't you apologize to me. No. You need to apologize to the Lord for the mess you made. And you're going to have to explain to Ms. Suarez about what you did. And before you go there, you go into that room and you apologize to that child and to your sister for putting them in harm's way. Do you hear me?"

"Yes, ma'am."

"And then, when you done with that, you go visit your father downstairs. You are not to leave this house for two weeks. You understand me?"

"Yes, ma'am."

Me and Rhea both gulped; we knew what that meant.

The door to the bedroom opened slowly. Wendy walked in. The brightness from the window showed just enough light to show the glistening tears on her face. First she went over to Rhea, kissed her on the forehead and said, "Hey, girl, I'm sorry, okay?"

"Uh huh." Rhea hugged her. They were close. All of them. But the two sisters had such a bond even though they were years apart. You could feel it.

Wendy walked over and sat on my bed, just like her mother had. "Carmen, angel girl, I am so sorry I left you alone. I am so sorry." And she started crying all over again.

"Wendy, I'm sorry. I really am."

She almost laughed through her tears. "What are you sorry for? Having good hair? Being a Spanish girl with pretty colored skin? You didn't do anything wrong. You have nothing to be sorry about. Now go back to bed."

"Canela," I whispered. "I am the color of cinnamon. In Spanish, it's canela."

Wendy pushed me lightly back under the covers and tucked me in. Then, looking back only once, she walked out the door.

Minutes later we could hear Mr. Watson yelling. His anger was fierce, but the disappointment in his voice was harder to bear. "What the hell were you thinking? What if that little girl got seriously hurt or even killed? I thought you were smarter than this, but God forgive me for not raisin' you right!" Every time Wendy would go to answer, Mr. Watson would jump in again, "Shut your mouth! I'll let you know when I want you to answer!" All you could hear from Wendy now were whimpering mumbles.

I started to cry as I heard what sounded like her taking another hit. Rhea was crying too. I got out of bed and crawled into Rhea's. We both huddled next to each other all night, listening to Wendy take her punishment.

The next day my wounds were a bit worse than the night before so we got to stay in bed and watch TV all day. I got to talk to my mother on the phone that morning and she said it was alright for me to stay for a few more days till I healed a little better. I got treated like a queen for three days! Rhea and I played in her room and Wendy even got us that ice cream she had promised us.

Eventually, my hair grew back and my scars healed. The physical ones for sure, anyways. It'd be a very long time before I could understand what it meant to be Black—or White, for that matter.

The mistake people make is assuming that the word Black only means African American. It does not. Just like the word White doesn't just mean Irish American. Being Black or White is about how people perceive me based on the color of my skin. It has nothing to do with where my family is from, my culture, or my ethnicity. It's just visual. All about skin color.

I'd always been a Black girl. A Latin girl with dark skin. But I'd never pretend to be African American. I would never disrespect the Watsons or my mother by not understanding the difference.

* * *

I tried to find Mrs. Watson again many years after Mama had died. I knew she might be the only person alive who could help me find you, learn about you. She was Mama's best

friend, and if Mama had told anyone about who you were, I'm
sure it would've been Mrs. Watson.

I didn't have much luck at all.

It was a fleeting thought anyways. Every once in a while I'd
wish I could find you, and then I'd realize I didn't want to
really find you as much as I just wanted to know you.

Janine

Boston was so sectioned off back then. In a lot of ways
I loved it, just the way it was. You knew where you could
go, what time of day you could be there, and for how
long—completely depending on just the color of your
skin. For example, if you were White back then, you
wouldn't dare show up in Roxbury after dark by yourself.
And, similarly, if you were Black, you wouldn't show up in
Southie (South Boston) after dark by yourself either. And
it was all based on nothing but skin color.

If you didn't have a strong idea of who you were, that
alone could mess with your sense of self. That alone could
determine your future on the streets. So many people I
knew were racist, but they didn't even realize it. Some
people would say right in front of me, "That nigger
shouldn't be in this town." Then they'd look straight at me
and say, "Oh, well, you know you're not really Black,
Carmen." I'd shake my head, because I didn't really know
what else to say or do. I wasn't going to make myself Black
in the one end of town that I danced in, or make myself
kinda sorta White in the neighborhood where I hung out.
So I did what any person in my position would do—I
learned to live in many different worlds.

I listened to AC/DC, The Rolling Stones, The Doors,
Queen, and The J. Geils Band when I was with friends in
West Roxbury. It was Grand Master Flash, Kurtis Blow,
Soul Sonic Force, and The Sugarhill Gang when I was in
Jamaica Plain, hanging on Forbes. I enjoyed corned beef

and cabbage, shepherd's pie and the like when I was with my White families, and could roll just as easily eating grits, fried chicken, okra and black eyed peas when I'd cross back on over to the Black side of town, known as Roxbury. My comfort food was *arroz y frijoles* and *platanos*, and, yes, flour tortillas when in Jamaica Plain with all my Latin-esque families, because it reminded me of Mama. My cinnamon-colored skin was a plus. That, and a good attitude, and I could fit in anywhere.

At the end of the day, I always knew I was the epitome of an American. My very own melting pot.

One of my best friends back then, Janine, was also a dancer and in Winter Guard as well. She was just as addicted to performing and was pretty good. She was quiet and stayed to herself, so naturally we became friends.

I never wanted to outstay my welcome anywhere. After all the drama over at the Lowells' that I had caused by dating such an ignorant animal, I found myself wandering the streets again and wondering where I might be able to go. Thankfully, I always had friends all over Boston. If I needed or wanted to stay somewhere, I just had to ask. But Janine didn't even wait for me to ask. She just told me to stop on by—if I didn't mind staying on the couch or the floor, depending on how many people were over. She had eight brothers and sisters. How could I resist?

Being a part of this family…let me just say, was unique, a privilege, even. It was an amazing place to be. Far from being a perfect model family, they were just so real and familiar to me. If they weren't all Irish, I'd swear they were just like every other Hispanic family I knew growing up. People were coming and going at all hours of the day, they all had jobs and contributed, but everyone had some sort of drama as well.

Mrs. McCullen, their Mama, had the sweetest disposition. Before she married Mr. McCullen she was a nun! So she was beyond kind and generous just in her demeanor. She really was one of the most loving, genuine people I'd ever met. She emanated joy when she walked in the room. And when Janine brought me home and asked if I could stay on the couch "for a while" because I had nowhere else to go, Mrs. McCullen didn't blink. She welcomed me as if I was a long lost relative and had always been part of the family.

Of course, as with any family I was ever a part of, I also participated in family chores, family meals, family discussions—but here it was far more fascinating. There was no schedule or list of chores anyone had to do. In a sense, it felt like there was no coordination in this family household. I would say it was pretty chaotic most days. But there was a sweet rhythm to it all nonetheless. Everyone was doing their thing, but there was a structure to it all, even if I couldn't figure it out. And there was love. So much love. Even when things were going bad or some tragedy happened, there was always a palpable love that lingered in that house and bonded them all.

Janine was this really beautiful girl. She had long, thick, brown hair that went down to her knees, green eyes, and tanned, freckled skin. She was also an amazing performer. We became friends at rehearsal, mainly because it seemed like we were the only two people in the organization who were not doing drugs at all. We both smoked. I smoked menthols, Newports, and she smoked Marlboro's but, other than that, we were pretty similar in our thoughts about drugs, performing, rehearsals and, well, about everyone else.

There were nights that we'd stay up laughing about how horrible someone else performed, or analyzing a competition that we lost, or just gabbing about the latest gossip. Janine was probably the first best friend I ever had after Rhea when I was just a little girl. Don't get me wrong, I had plenty of girlfriends, but Michelle and Julia were more like sisters. It was different. Janine was a good gossipy, lets-talk-about-boys kinda girlfriend. And when she liked a guy or I liked a guy, we both helped each other out to "get" the guy—or at least we'd try.

Janine worked at the Colonel Daniel Marr Boys and Girls Club in Dorchester. And, more times than not, she'd invite me along to hang out since I'd really have nothing to do, especially during the summer months when school was out. Eventually, she helped me get a part-time job working the afterschool daycare program. And that's when I had my first real crush on a boy from Southie—Ryan.

Maybe Ryan was nineteen, but back then he *seemed* much older. He was a supervisor or some "important" person who was in charge of a lot of stuff at the Boys Club. That alone made him seem much older than the rest of us.

Ryan was cool. Very cool. There was a certain kind of charm he had—that twinkly eye with the sparkly smile thing for sure. And he was also good looking. Very good looking, in fact—blonde, almost white hair, incredible blue eyes, very Irish, very "Southie" (meaning he came from South Boston, the "wrong" or "other" side of town, depending on your perspective). He seemed stern at times, very strict, but connected with all the kids somehow. He had a kindness about him that underscored his bold authority. He was liked by everyone, especially the girls. I pretended to never notice him or be affected by his presence whenever he walked into the room. But there was no doubt I always knew where Ryan was and, if I didn't, I always found out. Just so I'd know.

Secretly, I admired him, thought about him, was "in love" with him. As much as a teenager can be in love, I suppose. My heart skipped a beat whenever he was around, and I dreamed about him constantly. Janine knew how I felt about him. She thought I was nuts, but always understood there was something between us. We'd barely talk. I'd avoid him most days—the telltale sign of when I was interested in someone, Janine would say. And yet, when Ryan and I did talk, our conversations were always filled with sarcastic quips, funny-isms, and silly jokes going back and forth. I kept my words to a minimum with Ryan, kept my distance, but our glances across the room, our locked eyes and smirks, told of a far more intimate friendship, a deeper relationship—at least in my mind anyway. He was the first boy who ever got inside my head that way.

I remember one evening a bunch of us were hanging out in front of Janine's house—a common occurrence in this neighborhood—but this particular night was special. We had all been sitting on the porch late into the chilly, fall evening, talking and gossiping about something when, to my surprise, Ryan showed up with a couple of other boys from the club. He was wearing dark jeans, a black turtleneck, a leather jacket that he left unzipped even in the cold air, and a scarf dangling around his neck. I had seen him in the distance before anyone else and watched him kick away the colorful leaves that had fallen from the trees. He stepped up to the porch and grabbed a drink from one of the other girls, who willingly offered, and then chimed in to the conversation. I remember staring at him from the side of the porch, staying quiet and wondering if he'd even noticed me. I remember wishing it had been my drink he had taken instead of hers.

The evening went on and I kept my distance, talking to everyone else but him. Laughing when I was supposed to, though never really paying attention at all, secretly watching Ryan's every move, dreaming of the possibilities. I watched the girls flirt with him and wondered if he liked any of them. Wondered if he could ever like me. Every so often, I'd catch his eye and then, shyly, I'd look away as if I hadn't been looking at him at all.

Eventually, people left as the night was getting colder. Janine walked in to grab the phone and one of the last girls followed her in. Finally, there we were, Ryan and me, alone at last. I was leaning against the porch railing and he looked straight at me and I stared deeply right back.

Without saying a word, I started to walk past him to go into the house and I brushed up against him. He grabbed my arm and turned me towards him. I pushed him away. He pushed me back. I stumbled off the porch and fell to the ground. As he went over to help me up, I grabbed his legs and knocked him down. We wrestled back and forth, laughing, smiling, rolling in the leaves. At one point, I had him pinned and, as he lay beneath me, I saw him smile and I thought I had won. But just as I smiled back, he pushed me over easily and pinned me down, holding down both my arms. With the weight of his entire body on mine, I tried to move my leg, and he pressed against me harder. He stared at me. I stared back. No more smiling.

The leaves fell slowly behind him. It all seemed like slow motion. His face was moist with sweat. We were both breathing heavily, rhythmically. His stare was deep. And I was comfortable. Completely comfortable. I didn't flinch or shy away. We were connected and my eyes fixated. I knew everything I needed to know. It was all perfectly clear. He moved closer. I welcomed it. Just as our lips were to touch, just as his lower lips almost brushed mine, he quickly pulled away. He let go of my arms and rolled off of me. He stood up quickly and extended his hand and helped me up. We both brushed the leaves off of our clothes and he took the last leaves out of my hair.

In the driveway a car had pulled up. It was Janine's older sister, Megan, and her boyfriend. Megan called over to Ryan and asked where Janine was and Ryan responded, "Inside." And that was it. The moment was gone.

Ryan didn't say goodbye, but he didn't have to. I knew he had to go. He brushed my cheek with his hand and then walked away, looking back only once.

For years, I was in love with Ryan. I'd find myself in Southie for any reason at all, in hopes I'd run into him or his brother, Richie, who also worked at the Boys Club. But knowing Janine's family and Ryan's family was all I needed to feel comfortable in South Boston. I loved going down the boardwalk to grab a hotdog at Sullivan's. Or to just sit on a bench there and gaze out along the water. Of course, secretly, I always hoped to run into Ryan, but it never happened. At the Boys Club it was obvious he liked me and that I liked him, but both of us knew there was never, ever going to be anything between us. Girls from Jamaica Plain don't date boys from Southie. And boys from Southie don't date Black girls, period.

The Boys Club was a safe haven for me in so many ways. I was comfortable. I'd made it out of high school, was living with the McCullen's, and was working more than part-time—and, the best part, I had family and friends all over Boston.

But performing had taken its toll on me in so many ways. My hard training and years of injuries had rendered my body less willing and able to continue dancing. I started thinking I had no real alternatives, so I quit.

I was depressed about it. I didn't realize it then, but I was. I thought it was a cruel joke from the Gods above. I tried to teach and choreograph, but teaching clearly wasn't my thing. I wanted to dance, to perform. And now, this part of my life was over. I walked away from all of it. Cold turkey.

Janine tried to be supportive. At one point, we had an apartment together, the following summer, in Dorchester, not too far from the Boys Club, but it didn't help. We were roommates, and worked together, and the best of friends, but I was getting sadder and sadder. Life felt directionless and worthless.

Nothing made me feel better. I'd go to AA meetings, hang out with old friends in all parts of town, and I kept feeling the walls closing in. If I couldn't dance, if I didn't have family, if I didn't have school, who was I?

I wanted something else…maybe something more.

* * *

I tried to kill myself twice…and it was your fault.

The first time, I swallowed a bottle of someone else's prescription pills. I remember feeling extremely weak and falling to the ground. Then I woke up with a tube down my mouth as I gagged myself awake. My stomach had been pumped.

The second time, I jumped out of a window.

I landed headfirst with my leg dangling on the wire steel fence, caught on one of the twisted spikes in the wire. I bled everywhere. I was rushed to the hospital and had eight stitches. I couldn't even get dying right.

There were rumors that when I was a baby you showed up at the hospital when I almost died of an asthma attack. The story goes you tried to see me, but Mama wouldn't let you. And since you weren't listed on the birth certificate, the doctors had security show you out.

There's another rumor that you were definitely Italian. But the basis of that rumor has more to do with you throwing spaghetti at Mama or making spaghetti for Mama—no one seems to remember the story straight when they try and tell it, and no one seems to know more than that. But it's all I've got.

You should have looked for me. You should have fought for me.

You should have cared for me. You should have been there for me.

You should have been there for her. You should have cared.

I was tired. I was eighteen years old and I'd done everything right, but everything kept turning out wrong. And I just didn't know what else to do.

Anthony

I met Anthony on the bus one day when it was raining. He'd obviously been standing out in the rain for some time waiting for the bus when he walked on. He was drenched.

I handed him a bunch of napkins I had in my duffle bag—I was heading out again to someone else's house to sleep so I had plenty of the basic necessities I needed to get by. He said, "Thanks." And that was it.

A few days later I saw him again on the same bus. He was very dry this time. He sat right next to me and thanked me again for helping him out.

He wasn't too good looking, though he would have been if he weren't so thin. He had a real long face, sunken cheeks, and a real lanky way about him. I found him intriguing. There was a shine about him. An inner joy. Other people, well, they might have thought him weird.

We saw each other on the bus quite often after that, and, eventually, one night we decided to meet at Boston Boston, a dance club near Fenway. The name had long since changed to something else, but that's what the people "in the know" still called it.

When I walked in, it was beyond crowded. Wall-to-wall people and so much drinking and smoking it was tough to imagine I'd find Anthony at all, let alone be able to dance with him.

And then, as I sat at the bar alone, people watching, I just, well, saw him. He was one of the dancers in the cages. I would have never believed it, but it made total sense. He saw me looking at him and he did a special little routine up there just for me. It was fantastic!

Later that night, when Anthony's shift was done and the party was still going strong, he came down and sat with me at the bar. I'd been getting free drinks all night, just from knowing him, but when he came back down and sat with me, he also ordered us some champagne. I asked him if he was trying to get me drunk.

"Honey, I don't think I have to try. I think you're already halfway there, my sistah."

He was right. I'd been drinking up a storm. I wasn't drunk, but I wasn't going to be ready to drive any time soon either.

"So, Anthony, what are we celebrating?"

"Gurl, pahleeze. How could you NOT know? Your new life. Honey, once you meet Anthony your life is surely to change. Guaranteed. One hundred percent."

That actually scared me more than he realized, but I drank the champagne when it came nonetheless.

As the crowd thinned out a bit and I started feeling a bit more at ease, I asked the DJ to play Irene Cara's "Flashdance." After a few songs the beginning started, and Anthony motioned for me to take the floor with him.

He didn't know I was a dancer. Or that I used to be. And so I started, taking off my heels first, and then slowly moving from the corner of the dance floor. As the music played I was again outside, dancing in front of my house under the street lamp light, barely seeing the shadowy crowd in front of me.

It was magical.

Anthony was beside himself. And when the song finished and I landed my final turn on the other side of the room, he came running over and hugged me. The few people left in the club clapped and whistled, bringing me right back to reality.

"Gurl! You've been keeping that from me! Now that was something."

I couldn't stop smiling.

"Carrrrmengseeta baby, you're a dancer! You should dance. I can get you a job here."

He helped me up.

"Anthony. I'm not a dancer anymore. I'm done. I'm hurt."

"Honey, we all hurt. That's just life. You just need to work around the hurt. You know what I'm sayin'? Enjoy it while you can."

I laughed. He was so happy. "I don't know. I love it, Anthony, but I can't do it anymore. It hurts too much. The pain after a few hours is almost unbearable. I almost don't want to either. If I can't do it the way I want to, I'd rather just keep the memories. Does that make sense? And then I can have cool moments like this."

He lit a cigarette. "Uh huh. Sure does make some sense." He took a long haul. "But you got too much in you to sit back and do nothing. Look at you. You're like a pretty little wrapped gift with a sweet surprise inside. How you not gonna share all that with the world? You've just got to share it, honey. Don't waste any more time."

"You're so funny, Anthony! I love hanging with you. You're something very sweet yourself. I'm glad we're friends!"

And just then Whitney Houston's version of "The Greatest Love of All" came on and we sang our hearts out, mostly out of key. It was a great night. A fun time. And a night I've never forgotten.

We spent a few more nights like that together at the club. But that night was so very special. It was something like a dream. Anthony kept encouraging me to find a way to keep dancing and I kept resisting. Wasting time. And then one day I stopped hearing from Anthony. I came to find out he had died. AIDS. It had only been a few months we'd known each other, and we had never discussed it, but when I think back on it, clearly he was sick. But maybe as his new friend, he enjoyed not having to discuss it at all. And with me, he was just another dancer. Another friend.

Certainly, I didn't know him long, but I knew him enough. A pretty little wrapped gift, with a sweet surprise inside.

I wasn't going to waste any more time.

* * *

I stopped feeling sorry for myself.

I wasn't mad at you at all. I wasn't mad at Mama either. I was just lost for a minute. I lost my way.

I had kept going to AA meetings and hanging with friends, but things had gotten hazy. Somehow I rationalized that not dying when I tried to kill myself twice wasn't that I had failed, but that God still had some work for me to do.

How did I miss all of it? I had been looking at everything wrong. I hadn't lost Mama. I had her for eleven and a half years. That's how I had to look at it.

And not having you? It was okay. Look at all the dads I did have. All the families I did get to be a part of. I hadn't done drugs. I hadn't gotten pregnant. I'd never been arrested. I graduated from high school. I made it through all of that!

And sure, the dancing thing, the performing thing, that was harder to settle on. But I figured I'd make sense of it later. I needed to find my way out of Boston. I needed a way to get a real job that would take me somewhere. It was a reach, a long shot, but I needed to try now.

I just needed to "work around the hurt." Thank you Anthony.

And to begin again…

Fenner Hudson Financial

Bink. James Graham.

Good looking. Beautiful.

He had the brightest blue eyes, light brown, blondish hair, his skin…flawless. He was tall and obviously worked out. When he smiled his teeth sparkled. In a word: stud. But to just call him a stud wouldn't do him justice. His personality matched his beauty. Based on his looks, you might guess he'd be fake, but he wasn't. Far from it. James, or "Bink" as his dear friends called him, for reasons I'm still unsure of today, was genuine. The real deal. Gorgeous and charming, but a sweet, sweet soul. Most women in the company wanted to date him. Most guys, I think, wanted to be him.

The first time I met James was during my interview for a job at a firm in the financial district in Boston, or as I called it back then, "Yuppieville." Yuppies were what we called anyone who had money back in the day—it was short for Young Urban Professionals. More specifically, white collar young'n business types. In my neighborhood, it meant anyone White with a car who wore a suit when they went to work, and that the work was "legit," of course. Something "office-y" and important, not selling drugs and such. And the financial district was loaded with 'em. Yuppies, that is.

It was my first real job interview. It'd be my first professional job if I got it. The newspaper ad said they needed an "experienced" administrative assistant. Well, I wasn't experienced, but I sure as hell knew enough about being someone's servant to cover the "assist," and after manipulating a few lines here and there on my just-created resume—enhancing or straight up lying about a set of skills—I sent it in. Surely I wouldn't get an interview.

To my surprise, a couple of weeks later, the Yuppieville folks called and scheduled me for an interview the next day. I scrambled to borrow a next-door neighbor's makeshift suit and shoes—a dark outfit she used mostly for funerals, she thought an important aspect to mention. I wore her fancy high heels that were too big for me, a skirt riddled with safety pins to hold the hem up, and I carried an old briefcase stuffed with magazines and a book I'd never even heard of, let alone read, to make it weigh something while I rode the train into uncharted territory. When I saw my reflection in the glass department store window as I walked on by, I couldn't help but see how real professional-looking I was. I was so proud of how I looked—in a suit and all. Look at me, a girl from the hood looking all important and stuff. And walking into this part of Boston for a real job! Who would have ever even thunk it?

Certainly once they interviewed me, once they tested me—especially the typing test—I'd surely fail. But still. I had nothing better to do and it was exciting. For all of us. My friends thought it was cool. And bets were being made if I'd get the job or not—most betting against, by the way. I didn't take offense at all. Shoot, I'd bet against me too. This was out of my league. College folk. Smart people. Rich White folk. Yuppieville. There was no way a hood rat was getting a job here, but it'd sure be fun trying.

Of course, what happened next would change my life forever.

I remember that morning like it was yesterday. After all the hoopla of just trying to find the right building, I finally found the right place. I walked up to the receptionist, who showed me to the conference room and told me it'd be a little wait. Before I could fully catch my breath, a woman walked into the room and the interview began. Her name was Sharon. Without even looking at me directly, she started asking me all sorts of questions which I had pretty much prepared for with my friends the day before. I had an answer (or a lie, actually) for most of her inquiries. Sharon was this lanky librarian type with out-of-date glasses and pasty, White, blotchy skin. She wore a plain skirt and a printed blouse, nothing fancy. She seemed nice enough at first, but there was something about her that rubbed me the wrong way. It could have been that she kept repeating that I'd be working for "her and only her." That I was being hired to help "her" and that I'd be answering to "her and only her." She'd be my direct boss. I remember thinking that the more she talked about how much I'd have to answer to "her and only her," the less impressive she seemed. What she didn't get was that I already assumed I'd be working for her. She was interviewing me, for goodness sake.

As far as I was concerned, Sharon was one of the yuppie folk. She had the great job and probably lots of money—although clearly she wasn't spending it on clothes—but she must've had some money and been real smart to be working here in the financial district in this fancy office. But the more power she tried to claim, the less I started to think she had. She reminded me of peeps on the street like Deon—always talking smack about how great he had it running shit for some gang bangers. Trying desperately to get you to believe he was so happy and doing fine. And yet, while he's talking you, you know he ain't nothing but a loser. A druggie working off whatever he smoked or getting credit for whatever he hoped to be injecting. I learned the line "thou doth protest too much" living in the hood. Jackson used to say it all the time. I used to say it under my breath about dumbass people like Deon. I wanted to say it to this Sharon chick as I sat there, but I didn't. I kept my mouth shut. I stayed professional. That was the goal.

But I digress. I was answering the questions pretty well when she asked one I was sure to fumble on. "So, it says here in your cover letter that you can type sixty-five words per minute. That's pretty good, amazing in fact. You also have computer skills. Excellent. I'll be testing your skills after the interview. How are you with dictation?" My heart skipped a beat. I wasn't completely sure what that was exactly and we hadn't talked about what to answer if someone asked about dictation. But the first words out of my mouth were, "Absolutely. I mean, I mean, yes. Yes, I'm great with dictation." But none of it was true at all. Dictation? The angst in my chest got tighter and my stomach starting churning. Good ol' fear. I could always rely on fear to show up every time. Surely, I'd fail every test. I'd make a fool of myself. I could barely type—I was a two-finger-key kinda girl. And as far as using a computer was concerned, we had one in high school for about thirty kids. I knew how to turn it on, maybe print something but, other than that, I was totally confused as to what a floppy disk was and how it worked and such. My chest tightened. I was busted. Somehow I'd have to excuse myself from the interview and explain that I had some emergency or something when the testing part came.

And then it happened.

Clearly, something big had already happened. I just had no idea.

It was Monday, October 19, 1987. Of course, in hindsight, I realize it was Black Monday. In the financial world, it was one of the worst days when the stock markets crashed around the world. Now, back then, I didn't know this at all. I had no idea. To me the office seemed like a hustling and bustling type of place with an air of doom and gloom in it. I didn't think anything of it. This was a whole new world to me. I just assumed this was corporate-White-folks normal. Maybe yuppies were happy after they worked because they had all that money to spend, I didn't know. But I didn't think anything different was going on—that some major emergency had happened and that the world had stopped. Ironically, the stock market crash would be my saving grace—the stock market crash and James "Bink" Graham.

The conference room door opened and James walked in. He looked briefly my way. "Hi. Sharon, Edward wants to see you."

Without lifting her head, Sharon answered, almost under her breath, "I'll be out in a minute, Jim. Tell Edward I'm almost done here, please."

There was an awkward moment and then Jim interjected again, "Um, with everything going on right now, I think he needs to see you sooner rather than later. I'll take over here. No problem." He came up close to where I was sitting at the table and leaned up against it. "Hi, I'm Jim…or James."

I giggled, though I'm not sure why. A hot, tall White guy in a tie is still a hot guy, and he was talking to me—giggling was inevitable. I kept my composure. "Which one should I call you? Jim or James?"

"Doesn't matter. And what's your name?"

"Carmen. Nice to meet you." We shook hands. I couldn't stop looking at his smile. It was addictive. Immediately I felt at ease.

Sharon's pale face turned red. She seemed annoyed, and was attempting to keep her frustration bottled up inside, but that pale skin starting looking blotchier. White pale skin can be such a tell like that. Blushing or anger just doesn't show up the same way on Black folk's skin as it can on White folk's. I felt a little bad for her but, I can't lie, I was kinda glad she was getting pushed a bit by someone else. She'd been more than condescending to me during the whole interview. I know it's bad, but I kinda liked watching this James guy knock her down a peg. And he wasn't even trying. Obviously, he was above her in the pecking order of this office. And I could tell he already liked me. Very cool.

With that, Sharon excused herself and slowly got up from the conference room table. She grabbed her leather folder and made her way out the glass doors.

Jim made himself comfortable in the seat next to me. He didn't sit at the top of the conference room table as Sharon had, but pulled up a chair right next to mine. He was relaxed and easygoing. He grabbed my resume from the table and quickly scanned it. After a few seconds he put it down and asked me to tell him a bit about myself. Something about him had put me at ease. Surely, he was good looking, but he wasn't making a play or being cheesy at all—he was just easy to be around. It was as if all the tension and fear I'd been feeling about the interview had walked out the room with Sharon, and I was just having a conversation with an old friend. What I didn't know at the time but would eventually realize, is that Jim was one of the top salesmen in the company. Being good with people, making them feel comfortable—what some might call "schmoozing"—that was his gift. He was so good at it. And it was never cheesy; it was always authentic. He was brilliant. He understood his gifts, his talent, and had found a way to making a great living at it.

Again, I digress.

About thirty minutes had passed, and Jim and I were laughing when the door to the conference room opened up again. It was Sharon and the much talked about "Edward." Edward was clearly the boss and on his way out of the office somewhere. He looked boss-like, wearing a suit jacket and tie, perfect blonde hair, glasses—definitely important looking. The only thing that might be off on the whole "boss" image was that Edward had kind eyes. If someone had asked me to draw a picture of a boss—a legit one, that is—I'd draw him. I could tell instantly he was more like James than Sharon.

Clearly, Sharon didn't approve of the comfort level and laughter in the room, but Jim stood right up and said to Edward, "This is Carmen. I think she'd be great." Edward offered to shake my hand. "Nice to meet you." In a now sweeter tone Sharon joined in, "Well, I haven't finished interviewing Carmen and we have a lot of testing so—" Edward cut her off. He looked directly at me and said, "Do you want the job, Carmen? Are you willing to come early, stay late, and do whatever it takes to get the work done?" I answered without hesitation, "Yeah. Of course. I mean yes." Edward looked over at Sharon and said, "With everything going on today, let's just get her set up as soon as possible over at HR, before they change their mind." Sharon was about to say something but she held back. Again, her face began turning that blotchy red; she was not happy.

Jim winked at me while Sharon scribbled an address on a piece of paper and handed it to me. She said, "Go to Human Resources in the morning and report back to me when you're done." I remember thinking I wanted to respond "Yessum master" but didn't. Instead I said, "Okay, sure. Thank you so much, Sharon. Nice to have met all of you. Thank you." I walked away from the conference room as professionally as possible, but when I got outside the building I almost skipped all the way home. Really. I was so happy. I was pretty sure I had just gotten a job—a big-time real job in a big time company, with a real salary and other benefits. I was gonna be somebody after all. Maybe even a yuppie! And, more importantly, I'd be working outside the hood. As long as they didn't test me for those things, I bet I could pull off the job and learn stuff really fast. How hard could it be after all?

The following day, in yet another borrowed, haphazard outfit (this time a green dress), I met the rest of the salesmen I'd be working for. It was nice to have already met one of them, James. And James seemed genuinely happy to see me—that was his style. He made you feel comfortable from the moment you met him. It was as if you'd been best friends for years. I think it was one of the reasons he was so good at his job. He could sell you anything and you wouldn't even know you were buying it. That, and his good looks and charm is what made the ladies love him. But for me, it would be entirely something else.

I'd been working for Fenner Hudson Financial (FHF) as an administrative assistant for about two weeks. Basically, I did anything I was asked to do—mostly anything Sharon didn't have time to do, or whatever the eight salesmen needed. I made copies, filed stuff, mailed out letters. I'd get them breakfast or lunch if they asked me too. Although I was getting more and more familiar with my surroundings and what I needed to do, there was no doubt I was still way out of my element. Let's face it, a girl from the hood who'd never even worn a suit or been in a real office environment would always feel awkward, especially amongst a group of white collar financial types. But I kept it all inside. I kept it to myself, and I kept doing the best I could, using my newness to the company as an excuse for any mistakes I might have made. Sharon put up with me, but she clearly didn't like me. If it had been up to her, she would have never hired me at all. On this I have no doubt.

My inbox was piling up with a lot of computer-esque work I needed to do. Fact is, I was avoiding it. I didn't know how to use a computer very well and I think Sharon was beginning to catch on. I improvised and rolled with things as best I could. But I figured, at some point, something would happen and I'd get caught and lose the job. I didn't really care. Getting to this point alone was an accomplishment for a girl like me. I'd already gotten one official paycheck—more money than I'd ever seen legally in one lump sum—and it was all mine. I was sure I would get at least one more check. If they fired me, it would suck. But either way, I'd still be fine. I knew it was just a matter of time. I was sure of it. I didn't belong in this yuppie, white collar world anyway. I worked every day knowing that at any moment I'd be figured out and ultimately fired. It's what made logical sense to me.

One day Sharon walked over to me in the copy room and said smugly, "I've put work in your inbox and you still haven't done it. Are you unable to handle the work? Because if you aren't, we can get someone else to do it, Carmen." She always threatened me like that. She didn't offer to help, she just offered to replace me. "Um, no, Sharon," I said. "I'm sorry, I just didn't know what you wanted me to do first. Would you like me to be doing something else instead of copying these manuals you said needed to be done ASAP? I'm happy to do whatever you need or would like me to do." And she looked at me stumped. My ultra-sweet, syrupy kindness threw her. I think she was waiting for me to explode or go all "ghetto" on her or something so she could fire me for that, but instead I'd try and treat her like the god she needed to feel like so she'd have no recourse. Blind bitch. If she had had any street smarts at all, she would have easily seen I was working her—idiot.

Toni, the receptionist, who happened to be in the copy room at the time retrieving some documents for someone else, smiled (if not laughed) a bit, pretending not to hear a thing. Toni understood. Sharon cleared her throat and grabbed something off a shelf. "No, no, Carmen. You go right ahead and finish copying those manuals. But afterwards you need to do all five hundred letters and mailings to the contact list I put on your desk today. Those have to be mailed out tomorrow. So make sure you get those done no matter what." She started to walk away and then stopped at the door and said snidely, "Good luck." Toni looked at me and mouthed the words "what a bitch" and went back to the front desk.

I hated Sharon. She knew. She knew I didn't know how to use a computer. This was her original test that was delayed, but she was going to get it. She knew I could never get those letters and labels done in time. She was setting me up to fail and I knew it. As much as I didn't care about losing this White-world bullshit secretarial job, I did care about my pride. I wasn't going to let some gangly, dumbass librarian type make me look like a fool. So I had to come up with a plan. Somehow I had to get all the letters and mailings done before tomorrow morning. I could then throw them on her desk and tell her to kiss my Black ass and walk out of the office with my head held high. Fuck this dumbass job! It was only temporary anyway.

So that evening, when everyone had left the office, I snuck back in. I got to my desk and pulled out the list. It was pages and pages of names and addresses. I turned on the computer. After trying earnestly to figure it out, I realized there was no way I was going to understand how to do a "mail merge." Sharon had mentioned I should do that after I "input all of the addresses" so I could easily print them out but, obviously, when you don't know how to do something, you don't know how! Period. So, my next plan was to just type out each envelope one by one on the typewriter and then send a generic letter to each of the contacts. She'd never know. I could just copy them on the copier. I would seal each letter and bring them over to the mail room myself. I could then come back and quit—still telling her to kiss my Black ass. Good plan.

But, I wasn't a great typist. And by 10:30 p.m. on a Thursday night, I had still only finished about fifty envelopes. At this rate, I'd never be done in time. I'd used up a lot of whiteout. I sat there, occasionally staring out the window, noticing the bright moon glaring down through the skyscrapers that lined the city. What a pretty sight, I thought. For a minute, I pretended I belonged there. This was my office. My division. My department. I was a yuppie. It's rare when it happens, but I laughed and felt the tears well up in my eyes. No matter how I sliced it, she would win. Even if I got to tell Sharon to kiss my Black ass, I knew it was lame. I was nothing but a kid from the other side of those skyscrapers and I certainly didn't belong here. Damn. I did care. I did want the job. I liked getting a real paycheck. I liked putting on fancy clothes to go to work, even if they didn't belong to me. I liked being around these rich, smart, yuppie guys. And even if she hated me, everyone else liked me a lot. They thought I was funny and nice. And the best part—none of them knew anything about me at all. No one felt sorry for me because I had grown up the way I did. They didn't know anything about my past. For all they knew, my family was just like the friggin' Huxtables. And I was helping them with something important on Wall Street. At least I thought I was—I still hadn't figure out what they did, exactly, but it was important and legit. But the very best part—I was "making it." I wasn't working at the grocery store, or a fast food joint, or the Boys Club. I was working in the financial district in Boston. Mama would've been proud for sure.

I held back the tears and kept trying to type out the individual envelopes. I heard a noise and at first I stopped typing. Then realized it was probably just the cleaning crew—who I had always felt much more comfortable around anyway and I knew they'd understand why I was there. For a second, I wondered if one of them would know how to use a computer…maybe I'd ask.

When I looked back, it wasn't the cleaning crew. It was James. I turned back in my chair and stayed still. He was singing something or other and, before I had a chance to think about hiding, he noticed me and walked on over. "Hey, what are you doing here so late, Carmelita?" It was the first time he called me that. His voice was cheery. His Boston accent was thick when he said "Carmelita," as if the first part was the candy. I froze. I didn't say a word. I sat there, motionless, with my fingers on the typewriter keyboard.

He came closer.

"Carmel-i-t-a, did you hear me? What are you doing here so late? I had a bad date. Eeeh, it was okay, I mean, she was nice, but it was bad if I'm here, right?" He laughed out loud.

My chest was pounding so hard. I didn't think of this scenario. Nightmare. Imagine when Sharon finds out I can't type? She'll enjoy telling James that it was his fault. That hiring me was his mistake. And Sharon would tell him, "I told you so." This was so horrible.

James walked closer and touched the back of my shoulder. He turned me around and the tears, though not rolling down my cheeks yet, were certainly just about to flow.

"What's going on? What's wrong?" He looked around the table. He turned his head and saw the trash barrel full of torn-up envelopes and messed-up letterhead copies. He looked at the list next to the typewriter.

"Carmen. Why don't you just print these out from the computer? That would be so much easier."

I blinked, and the tears streamed perfectly down my face. And he knew.

"You don't know how to use a computer, do you?"

I didn't have to say a thing. I just looked at him quietly, humbly, my heart pounding, my hands shaking, tears hitting the corner of my mouth now.

"Why didn't Sharon just show you this list on the computer? She could've just shown you in five minutes how to mail merge this with the letter and then to the labels. The hardest part would be putting them in the envelopes and licking them shut." But as he asked the question, he knew the answer.

He walked over to my desk and turned the computer back on. He scrolled though a few things on the screen and found the same list I had been working on in a file. "Carm, come here. I'll walk you through this, okay?"

I gave him my chair and pulled another over. He moved the cursor around a few more times and then closed everything and started over. "Ready?"

"Uh huh," I said meekly.

He handed me a tissue. After a brief hesitation he asked, "Carmelita. Do you want this job?"

"Yes."

"Then, when you need help, you're going to have to ask for it. Do you understand me?" He wasn't cheery now, but spoke like a stern big brother, his tone just like Jackson's.

I didn't say a word. I shook my head yes.

He turned around in his seat and looked directly at me. "Look, I know it's been hard. You got hired at a crazy time. And Sharon probably isn't going to go out of her way to help you because she's…real busy…okay? And maybe you're not her favorite person. She's just jealous of you. You get that, right?"

I felt my eyebrows cringe together—that made no sense. "She's an Executive Secretary, I'm just a gofer. I work for her."

"Is that what you think?"

I shrugged my shoulders.

Jim took a deep breath and turned on the printer. Annoyed, he went on, "Well, you're right; you're not an Executive Secretary. An Executive Secretary knows how to use a computer, I suppose. But those are skills you can learn, Carmelita." His voice got softer and kinder. "But what you've got—you can't learn that. You walk into a room and it lights up. It's why we all like you. It's also why some people may be jealous of you. And while we're on the subject, we're a team here. You don't work for Sharon, you work for all of us. Okay? We all work together. Edward would tell you that. Anyone would tell you that."

I was mulling it over. I knew what he was saying, but I didn't know what to say back. He added, "Look, from now on, if you don't know how to do something, just ask me. Okay? It'll be our secret."

"But why?" I asked, knowing that no one does anything for free.

"Because I want you to stick around."

"Okay. But what do you want in return?"

"Huh…What?" he asked almost shocked.

I chimed in with attitude, "Well, where I grew up, nobody does anything for free. What do you want in return for helping me?" I asked with a newfound power. I could negotiate my way through anything—this was something I could handle.

He thought about it for half a second. He put the letterhead in the printer, clicked a few things on the computer, and then turned around and said nonchalantly, "Well, where I grew up, sometimes you do things for people, Carmelita, just because you can."

I didn't say anything at all. I didn't trust that answer. I was still waiting for what he wanted in return. I was uncomfortable. In true James form, he grabbed my shoulder and said, "Come on, lighten up! You can pay me back by…I don't know…get me the name of that new girl in accounting on the fourth floor. You know, the one with the ponytail. Did you see her here today? Hot damn. She was kinda cute. How's that? Fair?" And, as always, James had disarmed me. I couldn't help but laugh out loud.

"Let me get this straight—you'll help me with computer stuff, and I just need to be your pimp? That works for me. You've got a deal!"

We both laughed.

"You know, Carmelita, my friends call me Bink."

"Yeah, I know. But I think I'm gonna stick with James. I don't want Sharon or anyone else getting freaked about me calling you Bink. By the way—nobody, no one at all, calls me Carmelita…but…you can."

That night James and I sat folding letters into envelopes till about 1:30 in the morning. We laughed and talked and talked some more. It would be James who would teach me things I needed to know. Simple things like how to use email, certain software programs, all things computer-esque. But he'd also teach me about the market and how it worked. He'd answer any question I had.

Sometimes he'd leave me pamphlets or documents or newspaper articles if he thought it might help me understand something better. James made me feel safe in a place I really had no business being. He believed I was smart enough, good enough, and worthy enough. It was the first time in all my life that anyone cared for me so much who didn't know anything at all about my past. I don't think James ever knew that.

I spent a lot more nights working in the office, learning and relearning anything James had taught me after that. Sometimes I'd run into him on his way to or back from a date and we'd catch up. Those were some of my favorite moments back then.

So, the stock market crash of 1987 was, in a way, my saving grace, my shot at a different kind of life. And because of James, I didn't fail—he didn't let me.

A year or so later, my life would change again in magnificent ways forever because of the boys at Fenner Hudson Financial. And when I look back on it all, I can trace the beginnings easily to this moment—the stock market crash of 1987 and James "Bink" Graham.

* * *

If Bink was my secret weapon to keeping my job, then David Erickson was my saving grace.

David, or "Dave" as he liked to be called, was this six-foot-two, dark-haired, sleek, elegant kind of guy. When I first saw him from a distance, he reminded me of Pierce Brosnan—that Irish actor who had a show back in the day called "Remington Steele." Hot. Both Pierce and David. They had the same kind of hair, same build, same coolness. David seemed extremely quiet, but not meek. His quietness was a style, not a fear. He was powerful in his demeanor. When he did speak, his voice was deep, commanding, yet seemingly comforting. He was the epitome of a man's man. When David talked, people listened. He didn't waste words. He was the National Sales Manager, whatever that meant, and even though this department was run as a team and Edward was the ship's captain, David was definitely his number one.

To say there was an immediate bond between me and David would be an understatement. The first day we met, I was being introduced around the office, and when I was brought to his desk, he didn't even look up. He was in the middle of a phone call. Out of habit, he automatically went to shake my hand, almost as an afterthought, and when our hands touched, something happened.

A spark. A moment. A flash. The truth is it seemed more like a rug-induced static shock kinda thing. So embarrassing! The person he was talking to became unimportant and he put them on hold as he continued to hold my hand. There was a definite connection. And then, too long a linger...

I was startled. I looked at him confused, embarrassed, maybe even suspicious. Still holding hands, he looked straight at me far more confidently. He smirked and then smiled completely (something I'd realize much later he did rarely). He made some random comment about the electric shock but I barely heard him. There were a million thoughts going on in my head—too much for one moment. I pulled my hand away quickly but awkwardly once I noticed it'd been there too long. He still smiled. I smiled back uncomfortably. I was fascinated.

For a while, I hoped it was a mad crush, and a soon-to-be love affair *that he wanted*—he was so good looking after all, maybe even dreamy. It didn't hurt that he was a bigwig in the company and, from my point of view, rich. I daydreamed about the possibilities with David—especially when I was on the train going to and from work. He'd come to my very posh apartment in Beacon Hill, take me in his arms, and, looking deeply in my eyes, kiss me. Somehow, though, just as the dream was getting good, just as he was about to kiss me, I'd realize that it would never work. Unless I was a White, blonde chick living in Beacon Hill, with an education, and good family lineage—clearly I'd have to be, for someone like that, for him to even look my way. How dare a Black Latina girl from the hood dream such a thing? So many things about it just didn't click. I tried to push the dream further in my head, but I could never get passed my hood thing and his rich thing.

So, the dream changed. I'd dream he was my long-lost older brother. Somehow, he had evidence that I was his missing little sister. And because his whole family had been searching for me for so long, he was grateful to have finally found me. And they'd decided, as it was only fair, that I be included in the large trust fund that was left after father died. Even saying "father" in my dream was funny.

Yeah, when I dream, I dream big. That's how Mama taught me.

It was silly of course, to think David Erickson and I were related. Clearly, we looked nothing alike at all, though it would explain why we connected so powerfully. It was my daydream. And it was plausible. I mean, I certainly have many Anglo features. If I thought Chico, the bus driver, was my father when I was a little girl, or that Mr. Petrozelli, my third grade teacher, could've been, this certainly wasn't that far off.

It explained the "reading of the minds," the "knowing." At some point, the brotherly dream overrode any real romantic feelings I might have had for him. Plus, if there was ever even a slight attraction on my part, it was easily smashed by his being married. He was happily married from where I sat.

Since we really weren't related, there was no rhyme or reason for our instant closeness. It's not something we ever discussed; it just was. I was perplexed, at times, by our relationship; things just happened naturally. We developed a language between us that needed no words. It was as if I'd known him my whole life. It was familial, brotherly, maybe best friend-ish? I don't know. It was difficult to describe back then except that I knew it was a good thing. A deep-connected thing. And I wasn't going to let it go. He was my boss, they all were, but somehow none of that mattered. There was something special between me and David, or as I called him, "Da-veed" (David in Spanish). It was obvious to us the day we met, and it would become very evident to everyone else soon enough.

I had gotten very comfortable in my office settings. With Bink on my side, even Sharon wasn't able to throw me most days. She always tried making things more difficult for me but, little by little, I was figuring things out. It helped to know that James, beloved Bink, was in my corner.

But something else had happened too. I was learning quickly. I was feeling better about being more myself, the "street" part of me, just letting my natural self be. It was a cool mix of a professional me and a comfortable me. And now I could see what Bink meant when he talked about my personality. I did enjoy being in the office. However it happened, I could make people feel good. I could help. I had the ability to make people smile. I listened even when I didn't know what they were talking about (financial markets and economics were so over my head). But there was something else happening here. Before this job, it was always about making a few bucks to just get by, to pay a bill, to buy food. But now, working was about something bigger. Something I'd never quite understood before.

Everything in my life up until that point was about immediate needs. Doing things to survive. That's all I knew, that's all I saw growing up. Everyone trying to make a buck, no matter what that meant—dealing drugs, trading food stamps, working as a garbage collector, being a housekeeper…the list goes on and on. You did what you had to do to survive. No one loved their job where I grew up. Working was a chore. No one looked forward to going to work either. It always seemed painful. But working in this office environment, this elite place, even if it was just as an assistant, I felt I was doing something important. My little job was helping make the world work through this stock market thing I was still trying to grasp. Somehow I made a contribution, no matter how puny it was, and my job was connected to something bigger than me. It didn't matter how true or relevant my work actually was to the big picture, that's how I felt. It was a satisfying feeling. Something I'd never found in the hood.

Being needed was a good thing.

At this point, I had gotten real good at anticipating all of the eight salesmen's necessities. Whatever it was they needed. Sometimes it was preparing extra research packets for them when they had a big important meeting or getting them a sandwich or coffee from the store next door. Sometimes it was just about leaving them alone if I saw they were too busy or making sure no one bothered them if they needed some space. I was in some sort of sync with the place and I was loving it. I came in early and stayed late. I was obsessed with learning and understanding and, even though most of it was still hard to fully understand, I always listened when I could or read whatever I was mailing for them. The more I learned, the better I was at assisting and taking care of "my boys."

Of course, with all this happiness and kick in my step, Sharon, my supervisor from hell, was not too happy about it. I would see her from the corner of my eye as I talked to one of the guys after bringing them a coffee. She looked at me with a bit of contempt. She'd attempt to do things to sabotage my efforts or take credit for things that she had nothing to do with. As much as it bothered me, I did my best to bite my tongue and let it go. I had come to know that if I waited long enough, there would be another of those blessed karma moments where she'd attempt to do something I would normally do and it just wouldn't be received as joyously. It's not that the guys didn't appreciate her efforts, but sometimes when you try too hard that's just how it comes across—like you're trying too hard! Instead of being who she was, she would occasionally try to copy me and most times fail at it miserably.

I always knew the goal was to be more yourself. Trying to be like someone else would never work. But, as horrible as it sounds, I would revel in those karma-Sharon moments. I loved it. She'd attempt to do something nice for the boys, doing it as a way to show me up, or to present herself as part of the team, or "one of the guys," and it'd get slammed right in her face. And yet, even though I'd revel in the moment and privately have a sweet laugh when it happened, in a lot of ways, I felt really sorry for her too. I just did.

Until one day.

One day, Sharon forgot to have me assemble the latest research packets for some huge project that the big wig vice president needed for some meeting in New York. The packets were for a presentation and included precise charts and diagrams that the vice president (whose name was Kenneth, and was someone I'd only met passing in the halls) had himself created. He sent them to Sharon with specific instructions for each of the thirty completely custom research packets he had wanted for that day.

By the time Sharon remembered, it was pretty much too late. In a controlled but condescending voice, she explained the situation and then enlisted the receptionist Toni and another intern from another department to help me get the packets taken care of as soon as possible. You could tell she was anything but composed on the inside. She was frantic. It was 1988. Even sparing no expense, it was still going to be extremely difficult to print the packets, make black and white copies internally, go to another building for color copies, collate the packets (forty-five pages each), and get them to wherever Kenneth was going to be in New York on time. Suffice it to say, she was screwed.

But there we were, the three assistants scurrying to get them done nonetheless. In a lot of ways, I loved a crisis. I was good in them. And in an office kind of way, this was certainly a crisis. Kenneth would be without his materials. It would make him look bad. And more than anything, there was a pride in making sure the vice president, or any of our guys in the company, always looked good. It didn't matter if I barely knew them or ever spoke to them; it was a team. The 6:00 p.m. last-chance deadline passed, and we didn't even have one packet ready. Sharon was making phone calls to an assistant in New York trying to get the word to Kenneth that the packet wouldn't be there because of some glitch with overnight mail. Lies. I remember thinking she wasn't even a good enough liar, so this clearly wasn't going to get her out of trouble, but mentally I gave her a B minus for the effort. I was being a little gracious. I disliked her something fierce, but in this moment, I still felt sorry for her. Her ego was completely based on being a stellar executive assistant who never made mistakes. Again, it was kinda nice to see her knocked down a peg or two, especially of her own doing. Yup. I mean, I felt bad and all, but I have to admit, I loved watching karma do its thing. Oh how sweet it is!

When Kenneth returned from his New York trip, he made his way straight to Edward's desk. Our office was a series of open cubicles. Unless you were actually in Kenneth's corner office, which was the only one with walls, or in the conference room, you could pretty much hear everyone's business. That's why most people, when they had a problem, or a personal issue to attend to, would do it in the conference room, which was pretty much soundproof (although all glass, so you still had to mind your visual Ps and Qs). But Kenneth didn't seem to have much time to make it to the conference room. Edward, the head of our sales team, had already been prepared and knew what was coming. The kind of person Kenneth was, by all accounts, the missing little packets would not be the demise of his trip. None of these guys would have made it this far in life if they couldn't get by without a few materials to do their "thang." In that sense, Kenneth reminded me so much of Jackson from back in the day. The way he walked into a room, there was an air about him. Tough, but not so much mean. You just don't become head of anything in life without knowing how to improvise. I was pretty sure even though Kenneth was just the head of this yuppie gang of rich, White boys, he did his very best, without packets and all, to "represent."

But to us lowly peons, we had failed. When Kenneth finished his conversation with Edward, giving him the heads-up on how everything went, he turned to leave, and then stopped when he noticed Sharon standing like a wounded animal. Kenneth first looked at Sharon and then over at me. "Next time, let's try to get my materials to my destination way ahead of time, okay?"

I shook my head slowly yes looking down to the floor. Truth is, that might have been the first time Kenneth had ever even noticed me, let alone spoken to me. It might have also been the very first time I'd seen him face to face. I knew who he was, and that he had curly brown hair, and that he wore glasses but, most days, I'd just seen him as a shadowy figure in his office. His smile was warm and friendly, not fearful at all. His aura seemed genuinely kind and not as scary as I'd come to believe. For the most part, I thought he seemed just like Jackson. Pretty cool.

I thought the worst of it was over. My head stayed down, and I expected Sharon to just apologize for the mistake and we'd move on. But as he took a step to leave, dumbass Sharon spoke in a desperate voice, "Kenneth, I'm real sorry. Carmen never got to making the packets on time and so we got behind. Before I noticed she hadn't sent them to New York on schedule, it was already too late. That's why they didn't show up, not because of the overnight service. I really am sorry about that. It won't happen again."

Kenneth now took notice of me. My face must've been about to explode, which he misinterpreted as guilt, but clearly for me it was anything but. He said, "Not a problem, Sharon. I know your work. We still got the deal so it's all that matters." Looking at me directly he added, "I'm sure it'll never happen again." And he walked away.

Kenneth walked just far enough away not to hear me and I was about to blow. You could sense it. I could feel my neck tense, my shoulders straighten. My clenched fist and the apparent smoke coming from my ears were all a tell. And this time, it was going to be a violent one. Everyone in the room felt it, there was an unnatural quiet. I was done. If I had still been carrying, now is when I'd pull out my knife. Someone was about to get hurt. Bink tried to signal to me to calm down, but I didn't even acknowledge him. Nothing would stop me. She'd crossed the line and they all knew it. Blaming me for something I didn't do so blatantly was not acceptable. And I was about to make her realize how unacceptable it was.

I stood up, almost in slow motion. I turned around and focused like a laser beam on Sharon. She was scared. The words came flying out of my mouth and the ghetto kid from the streets was screaming. The expression on her face was as if I were talking in tongues. My hands were flailing as I clearly made reference to every single thing I ever thought of her. I heard snippets of people's voices attempting to get me to calm down, to stop, but nothing would stop my verbal assault on that woman. She was no longer my supervisor but some bitch from another crew who just tried to screw me. If she stayed quiet, my words alone would bring her down, but if she said one word, my fists to her face would do the rest.

In the midst of my tirade, just when I was seeing the tears well up in her eyes and I was about to go in for the kill, I felt a hand gently grasp my shoulder. Everything stopped for a moment. Only Mama could have touched me like that. It stopped me hard. My whole demeanor relaxed. My breath magically slowed. I remembered who I was supposed to be. Who I really was. I could feel her pressing gently on my shoulder and I anticipated the look of disappointment. Oh God, what have I done? Scared, I slowly turned around.

It was David. He grabbed me by both shoulders and looked straight down into my eyes. He was mad, disappointed. You could hear a pin drop. With his stern, deep voice he slowly said, "I need you to stop. Right now. Go into the conference room and wait for me."

I pivoted like a good solider and marched right into the conference room and waited. I was confused. I was shaken at the similarity of his touch. I just stood there. Looking at the wall. I didn't pace, but in my head I was running back and forth. How could this be? How did he do that? No one has power over me. No one can do that to me. I started wishing I had not been so stunned. I wished I had slammed the door when I walked into the conference room. I wished I had broken the glass—so much was running through my head. I was getting angry again. I was sure I had lost my job. I didn't care. Fuck these White people. And now I was about to get grilled for not handling the situation well. Or maybe I would just get fired. I should just leave now. I should just walk out and go back to where I belonged.

And just then David walked in. He closed the glass doors to the conference room and sat down.

"Carm, sit down."

I didn't move or even turn around.

And with a harsher voice he demanded, "Sit. Down."

"I don't wanna."

"It wasn't a question. Sit down…please."

I grabbed a chair furthest from him at the other end of the conference room and sat down with my arms crossed, looking at the table, waiting to hear what the great, White man had to say.

He stared at me for a long time and then, with a smirk, he leaned back in his chair and asked, "You hungry?"

"What?"

"I said, are you hungry?"

I was thrown. "No!"

"Well, I am. Let's go have lunch."

"What?"

"Carm, you're not mad at me. You're mad at yourself and we both know it. So, go get your coat, and let's go have lunch."

"I'm not hungry, I'm just mad, David."

He laughed a bit. "Aaah, so you are mad at me, you didn't call me Da-veed." He said it all wrong. His pretend Spanish accent was horrible.

I tried to sit there and be mad, but he kept staring at me from across the table. I didn't know if I should look at him or look away or at the table. I was fidgeting. He smiled from across the room.

I tried to take control of the situation so I blurted out, "I know you sided with her. I just hate that you would think I would ever make such a mistake or that she's so perfect. She's not you know. She messed up. And then she went and blamed it on me." My voice was getting louder. "And you know, I can take a lot of stuff, and I do. And I never complain. And then she goes and does that and embarrasses me like that? David, that's not cool. And I have no way to prove it. But it wasn't my fault. I can do her job and my job by myself, and most days I do! I'm so sick of this and it may not matter to you but—"

He cut me off. "Hey, stop."

Again I was thrown by something in his voice, something in his demeanor. He looked at me with such disappointment. He continued on, "You think I don't know what really happened?" He paused for a long time, shaking his head. "Carm, I was the one who sent her the materials for Kenneth's trip. I gathered those charts, research reports, and diagrams from the analysts and gave them to Sharon. I know you didn't have them. There's no way you would have known about the project. I reminded her about the packets two days ago and that's when I knew she'd forgotten." He leaned back in his chair. "Carmen." A moment passed. I didn't say a word or move. "Carmen. You don't trust anyone. You walk around with your guard up all the time. But we trust you. I trust you. We know who you really are and we all still love you anyways."

My head hurt. I didn't understand how he could be saying words like Mama would have said. I was confused. I stayed quiet, but I could tell David was concerned. He leaned back onto the table. "Look, I just told Kenneth and I just talked to Sharon about treading lightly next time she chooses to blame someone else for her own mistakes. Edward was sitting right there. Everyone knows it's not your fault."

"Really?"

He smiled. "Yes, really."

I waited a bit. "Am I fired? You know, for—"

He interrupted, "For going all wacko on her?"

"Wacko? Really? That's so very White of you, David I was gonna say going all 'ghetto' on her, but I guess 'wacko' works. And it sounds nicer, huh?"

He laughed. "Carm, what am I going to do with you?" He couldn't win either way.

"I don't know." I tied to laugh just a little.

"Carm, seriously. We need you here. I need you here. But you've got to work on how you deal with some situations. Keeping things bottled up inside is why you exploded the way you did. This wasn't about this one situation with Sharon. This was building up for a long time. In the future, you come to me, or Edward, or any one of us and tell us what you're upset about, or what's not working, and we'll figure it out. We'll walk you through it. I don't care who blames you for what. You keep holding things inside, you're going to blow up at someone again. And the next time, no one may be able to save you from yourself." He was so emotional about it. I'd never seen him like that. "Carm, You can always come to me for anything. Do you understand me?"

"Uh-huh." Was all I could muster. "Um, so…I'm not fired?"

"No, you're not fired." He said almost annoyed. He settled back into his chair and added, "Ever think of going to school?"

"What?" I was confused where this all coming from.

"College? Have you ever thought of going to college?"

I hesitated. No one had ever asked me such a question. "Um, no." I laughed uncomfortably. "I barely made it out of high school, not sure I'd get in anyways."

Without missing a beat he got up from his chair and said, "You'd get in. You should think about it. Let's go to lunch."

"You don't need to take me to lunch, Da-veed. I'm good." I got up from the conference table.

"It wasn't a question, Carm. We're going to lunch. So get your coat. And I'll meet you downstairs in five. Okay?"

I sighed. "OK."

We went to lunch at Matt Garrett's, the boat restaurant across the street. It was the regular hangout for our office, but also for other financial folk in the area. David and I spoke a bit about how to handle things in the future and his expectations of me. We didn't talk about this college thing at all, but it was in the back of my head now. I couldn't believe he thought I was smart enough.

We were there far longer than an hour. I watched him talk to all the other financial people who walked into the sports bar and greeted him like he was a rock star. Each time, without hesitating at all, he'd introduce me, "Oh, and this is Carmen, she's part of my team." They'd reach out to shake my hand like I was some financial analyst or someone important. I was so proud as I sat there.

That was the thing about David—he was proud of me even though I messed up royally. He had faith in me, even if I didn't. He thought I could go to college. That I could do anything if I put my heart into it. I realized as I sat there, he reminded me of Mama that way. He was tough, but always fair. Maybe he was my long-lost brother after all.

Later that afternoon, Kenneth called me into his office and apologized for not acknowledging how much work I had been doing since I had started at FHF. He hoped I'd "keep up the good work" and also gave me a raise. I was shocked to say the least. David had already given me a heads-up at lunch, but I didn't really believe him till it actually happened. And now I had this idea in my head that David thought I was smart enough to go to college. Me, a kid from the streets! I couldn't stop smiling about it. It might have been the best compliment I'd ever gotten. Surely I could do my job and Sharon's by myself, and most days I did most of the work that she took credit for anyway. College was never even a thought for me. It was for rich kids, rich, White kids at that. Graduating from high school was the only goal and, in my hood, that was hard enough. I didn't know anyone from the neighborhood who had gone to college. But it felt really good to think I was smart enough. And that David thought I could do it…well, that was just icing. It turned out to be a great day after all.

As far as Sharon goes, she never apologized. But from that day forward, she never crossed that line again. And neither did I.

* * *

It was a Monday morning.

The day had already started out hectic and it was raining. I missed the train, was running late, and knew I wouldn't make it in time to set up the conference room for the guys' regular Monday morning strategy meeting. It was just going to be one of those days.

As I walked off the elevator and into the lobby, Toni, the receptionist, motioned to me that the meeting had already started. She quickly whispered that she'd taken care of setting everything up for me—not to worry. I was gracious and promised to pay her back somehow. She replied, "Cool. Her Highness, Sharon, thinks you had a doctor's appointment." I laughed. Toni winked back, chewing her gum and answering her other line. Toni didn't have much love for Sharon either. It made me feel better I wasn't the only one.

I put my bag on my desk and started to change from my sneakers to my shoes when Sharon stepped into my desk area. She was being extraordinarily sweet to me these past few weeks and I wasn't quite sure what was behind it all, but I surely wasn't trusting it at all. Still in her scrawny outfit and librarian way, she stood there meekly by the separating wall and asked me how the doctor's appointment went and, was I alright? I continued Toni's improv and just told Sharon that I was fine and that it was just a pain near my shoulder that was not going away. "Nothing major but I wanted to get it checked out." She gently touched my arm and said, "Well, I'm so glad. You hang in there. Everything's going to be just fine."

I stopped cold. What? There was just something so phony about it. Her touch. The syrupy sweetness. It creeped me out. I don't think in the year and a half I'd been there she'd ever touched me even once. My interaction with her was so different from that of the rest of the office. Bink wouldn't even start his day without at least a big wave from his desk to mine and most times I'd walk over with my coffee and just check in for a bit. David and I had such a rhythm that it wasn't unusual to get a hug in the morning from him or, if he was sitting at his chair reading the paper, I'd walk by his desk and at the very least just mess with his hair a bit. He'd always reply, "Mornin',

Carm." It didn't matter if he was on the phone talking to someone; we'd get our morning hellos in for sure. It was just so natural.

I don't think Sharon had ever been able to be anything but "professional" with everyone. And when I say professional, what I mean is cold. She barely laughed most days and when she did, it seemed forced or uncomfortable for her. Certainly, up until that moment, she had never, ever touched me. Something was up for sure...

* * *

There was a rhythm to the morning with the boys. It was like a family in the kitchen before leaving for school. Everyone would say good morning and then there were just things you did before you moved on with your day. For example, as soon as I'd see Scot, one of the other boys in the office, we'd make plans to go downstairs and have a cigarette. Scot smoked much more than me, but that daily morning cigarette with Scot became our regular thing, even if I didn't actually smoke one with him. On bad days, it'd become a mid-morning, early afternoon, lunchtime, and hourly if-we-needed-it cigarette. Always right out in front the building, under the awning, no matter what the weather. It's where I got to know Scot best.

Scot was my confidant. Unlike James and David, Scot was the "normal" one. Normal in the sense that Scot could easily have been a "brothah" if he wasn't White. He was down to Earth, swore like a truck driver and talked un-yuppie-like when he wasn't around business folk. But he could throw it on in a moment—the professional charmer, the elite financial guru, the salesman. And then, just as easily, in the next instant, he'd be hanging with regular folk like me and not skip a beat. I admired that so much. I'd learned to be chameleon-like from him. Reading the environment correctly, adjusting accordingly. Armor from the streets was a protection, but the nuances of using

160

your strengths in different circumstances as needed was something I picked up from Scot. If there was anyone that made me feel like I could pull anything off at all, it was him.

Scot had really curly black hair. He kept it a little long in back and the curls would try to do their thing no matter how short he cut it. He had that perfect tannable skin, big brown eyes, and he always smelled good. It was like he'd just come out of a wonderful spring shower, but there'd be that hint of alcohol and cigarettes if you got close enough. Scot could drink anyone under the table. He was just one of those guys. Comfortable at the bar. Comfortable at a meeting with posh executives. I bet he'd be comfortable in my neighborhood too, hanging on Forbes Street. He was fearless. And although he loved his work, you could tell it wasn't his only priority. He seemed to love living life, period. From Scot's point of view, the world was his to enjoy—everything else was a means to enjoy it more. He was optimistic in general, a glass-is-half-full kind of guy. He would find a positive spin about everything, and he never seemed confused or uptight. I envied that about him.

Scot also had this great infectious laugh—a belly laugh that filled the whole room when he let himself go there. Like the other guys, if not more so, he always had my back. And if he ever needed it, well, I'd have his for sure.

I remember one time I'd been coerced into finally going to one of these infamous "company parties" that were always talked about around the office. It was being held by someone in the company who had a place on the wharf (these people were so rich!). Reluctantly, I went. I showed up by myself, hesitant to invite anyone I personally knew in case they misbehaved—but mostly because I wasn't sure how these folks would take to hood types. Normally, I would never go to these festivities since I always felt so out of my element, but Scot kinda dared me, and he knew daring me was a sure way to make me do pretty much anything back then.

It was late, and after finally finding my way to the building, there were two security guards or bouncers at the door. They were armed and really big guys. Certainly either ex-cons or Mr. Universe competitors. At first, I couldn't imagine this was the right place. But after watching a few other people walk in who I barely knew but was sure worked at the company, I realized this was the place after all.

I felt foolish and now nervous for showing up alone. I should have just met the guys after work and hung out with one of them till they left for the party—but goodness, that would have been hours, and even too much for me to bear. I couldn't have stayed at work much longer anyways. Sharon had been getting on my every nerve, so the minute it was 5:00 p.m., I was out the door and on my way home. I changed into yet another "work" outfit, and got back on the train headed to basically the same neighborhood to attend this party. I was cursing Scot under my breath for daring me to go, but clearly I was also intrigued, maybe even a little excited.

When I walked up to the door, one of the men asked me if I knew the password. I was shocked. I had no idea there was supposed to be a damn password! I said no and they grilled me for a bit as to why I was there. After a few minutes, someone else came up behind me and, although I'd never seen them before, they validated I worked at the company. Tweedledee and Tweedledum let me in.

I walked through the door and the hallway alone was beautiful. I could have lived right there, in the hallway, and been fiercely happy—that's how elegant it was. There was a chandelier that glistened, maroon textured fabric lined the walls, and a marble statue of some sort sat at the end of the hall. There were framed paintings along the walls, expensive, I'm sure. It was kind of awe-inspiring. I'd never been in such a beautiful place. The hallway was enough for me. But I could see that at the other end of it were two more doors where the party was. One side of the double doors was slightly open, and I could see figures moving back and forth. I could barely hear the music, but there was something playing.

I made my way to the end of the hall and walked slowly through the door. The room was filled with beautiful people. Strangers to me, but beautiful people nonetheless. I didn't know anyone here at all. And I was dressed all wrong. I started thinking that I was in the wrong place again. This was unlike any party I'd ever seen before. As much as I thought I should just leave, I couldn't help but keep looking around. It was loud, but not because of the music. People were just sitting and standing around talking, drinking and seemingly waving back and forth. There was an interesting smell, maybe familiar, but it was intertwined with too much perfume and ocean air. Most of the women were scantily dressed in beautiful cocktail dresses, and all the men seemed, well, dorky and businessy, and so out of their leagues.

Eventually, I did notice a few recognizable faces, but I wasn't sure. I was staring because they seemed familiar to me, but I couldn't pinpoint from where. And then, in a moment of panic, it hit me. Cops. They were cops. Pigs, as we lovingly called them in the hood. But why would cops be here? They almost looked human out of uniform. Still pigs though. They always took a strange pleasure in arresting the guys in our neighborhood for drugs or whatever else they could find. They were jerks. Crooked cops. And they were here at this party, as guests. It confused me. I kept walking around. People were laughing and smiling as if they were enjoying themselves, but something seemed so wrong, and I didn't know what.

In my neighborhood, a party was a PARTY. People danced till they were literally dripping sweat. There was always a DJ, and surely people drank and did drugs, but there was a festiveness to it. A vibe, of sorts. To me, a party was deep joy that seemed to permeate—until the cops came of course and busted it all up. But this seemed almost staged, fake somehow, people acting like they were having fun. Everyone seemed out of it and I couldn't...

And then I saw it. The coffee table. Mounds of a white powdery substance on silvery platters. Drugs and paraphernalia. It was better quality, I am sure, and definitely bigger quantities than I'd ever seen in my neighborhood, but it was the same basic shit nonetheless. I couldn't stop staring. And then the cop-looking guy walked over and did a line. I gasped and put my hand to my mouth.

Just as I was about to turn around and run out of there, an arm interlocked into mine—it was Bink. "Hey, Carm, we're all over here, in this room." I wish I could say I was happy to see him, but I wasn't. I had been hoping I had walked into the wrong party. But when we walked into the other room, the overwhelming stank of pot almost knocked me out. I was getting high just standing there. Everyone I knew from our department was there. They all seemed really happy—I mean, *overly* happy to see me. I was feeling ill.

Everyone was there and they all seemed drunk and out of their minds. Laughing and smiling for no apparent reason. A scene all too familiar to me, except it was normally in my neighborhood, not with people from my job. I didn't know what to say. I managed a quick hello and then, just as quickly, told them I was leaving because I was feeling sick. They seemed to be sad for a moment, till the next minute they weren't, and went back to their drinking and partying.

I would have run if it wouldn't have looked so stupid and if there weren't so many people in my way. Instead, I walked quickly, remembering my etiquette, excusing myself as I passed on by. At one point, one of the pigs slammed into me accidentally. He kept apologizing to me and I kept trying to avoid him seeing my face in case he recognized me and realized I wasn't supposed to be there. He'd know I was just a hood rat. I told him it was fine and I almost bolted out the front doors. The bigger bodyguard or doorman or whatever commented as I walked away, "Hey, that was quick." I didn't turn back. I kept heading towards the train stop till I heard someone yell, "Carm. Wait up."

It was Scot.

He grabbed my arm. "Hey. Wait up. Have a cigarette with me, okay?" We sat on a cement bench, still in view of the doors. He had a beer bottle in his other hand. He took a last swig and set it down on the ground. "Why are you leaving so soon? You just got here." He knew that whatever I said next would be a lie.

"Um…I just don't feel good. I shouldn't have come. I have a stomach ache."

He didn't look at me, but just kept staring straight ahead. "Really? That's what you're going with?" He lit a cigarette. "It's me, Carm. What's up?"

"Nothin'. Nothing at all. I just don't feel good." I couldn't look at him.

He waited a second. "You know, we're not perfect, Carm." He took a long drag of his cigarette. "You know we drink. Why are you so surprised by the drugs? It's not like you've never been around drugs, right?"

I took a long, deep breath. And still looking forward, I almost whispered in disappointment, "I know. God knows I know you're all not perfect." I laughed a little, but sadly. "And yeah, of course, I grew up around drugs, I'm around drugs all the time, but…"

He finished the sentence for me. "But this is the one place where you thought you were away from that?"

"No. I mean, yeah. But, Scot." I turned to him on the bench. "There were cops in there. I know it. And I have friends who've gone to jail for doing the same exact fucking thing." I sighed but continued on exasperated, "I bet I could tell you easily who sold you guys all that stuff just by looking at its packaging. And I bet the dealers who sold this stuff to these rich folk have been to jail themselves at least twice. How many of these rich folk do you think have been to jail for doing the same exact things my friends do in the hood? I bet none. It's not fair. It's just not fair. Rich folk get away with everything. It sucks. I don't know. I just didn't expect this. I'm sorry."

"First of all, I didn't buy or sell anything. None of our guys did. Sure, some of us may have smoked some pot, but no one was doing anything hardcore. Okay? That's why we were all in the other room. And secondly, what's wrong with you? You're smart. You know the world isn't black and white. There's a lot of gray in between. Of course things aren't fair. This was your first big realization of that? Come on. After the shit you've been through, you're just figuring out that life's not fair?" He took another long drag and with a softer voice he said, "Look, maybe there are cops in there, I don't know, Carm. But I wouldn't be surprised." He let out all the smoke in one big sigh.

After a long moment, I said almost under my breath, "I know life's not fair, I just—"

He cut me off. "You just thought we were all holier than thou. Perfect. See, we're not. We're *human*, just like you. Imagine that."

Embarrassed I said, "Yeah. Ugghh. I know. I'm an idiot."

"Naaah. You just got a good heart and a good head on your shoulders. You should do something with that brain of yours at some point. You're an optimist. That's a good thing."

I had no idea what he was talking about. I wasn't sure exactly what being an "optimist" meant, but I'd look it up when I got home if I remembered. I just went with it. A few minutes later, David and James came out of the party looking for Scot. When they got close enough, Scot told them I wasn't feeling well and we'd just come out for some air. I mentioned I was going to go home and James flagged down a cab for me. David shoved thirty dollars in my hand to pay for it. As Scot put me in the cab, he said, "You know, Carm, no one's perfect, but we're pretty close. We're the good guys. And when I say 'we,' I'm including you too." He shut the door, smiled, and blew those smoke rings out his mouth as he waved goodbye. I smiled, not feeling so upset anymore.

On the ride home I wondered about it all. How unfair life really was. Not just for what happened at the party versus my neighborhood, but even my whole life. I had never thought about how unfair things had been even for me. Up until that point, I just accepted that this was the way things were. I had to play the cards I'd been dealt, period. I had to survive. But now I was thinking so many thoughts. That these guys weren't really that different from the boys on Forbes street after all. And that maybe I could go to school? Maybe things weren't so black and white. I wasn't sure. But something had happened that night. And Scot had me realizing that no matter what cards you've been dealt, you always control the choice on how to play them.

* * *

One Thursday after work, everyone decided to stop by the unofficial FHF hangout next door, Matt Garrett's. Ever since coming here with David that day after I blew up at Sharon, I'd come to love this place. All the guys were there and people from neighboring offices went there for drinks after work as well. I always felt a little out of place, but there was also something about being there that made me feel good too. I loved seeing the guys being total idiots around women or talking about sports instead of the bond market. It was kinda fun. I'd become one of the boys—or maybe just part of the background. Either way, they seemed to feel comfortable being themselves when I was

167

around. Surely alcohol had a lot to do with it, but it was always still a lot of fun.

It was getting late. James had already left to go home though, like the rest of them, he'd had way too much to drink. It had been a fun night of them talking about things I had no idea about, but I just kinda sat at the bar and watched. I talked to a bunch of people, watched and listened, and ate some fries as I nursed a daiquiri. In my own way, I was having fun.

At some point, I noticed the time and realized that if David didn't leave soon he wouldn't make the last ferry home. I pulled him away from the group and told him he needed to get going. He didn't question me at all; he just grabbed his coat and started walking out the door. He was clearly drunk. Not off-his-rocker drunk, but certainly he had had way too many. I decided I'd walk him down to the ferry to make sure he made it. At first, when he realized I was walking with him, he looked at me strangely and said out loud, "Okay," as if I had asked if I could walk him. He mumbled something else and I told him I couldn't hear him. So he asked again, "How are you getting home?" I lied and said I was taking a cab. I knew it would put him at ease, but I'd take the train. These guys spent money like it grew on trees. It really wasn't that late to take the train, and I certainly wasn't drunk.

We were close to the ferry and would easily make it in time, even though David was walking rather slowly. I was talking about something or other when I finally noticed David had stopped walking. I stopped and turned back to him. It'd just been a few steps. As I made my way towards him I noticed he was mumbling something, but I couldn't understand him. I got close enough to hear him, and just as I was about to ask him what he was saying, he leaned in and kissed me on the lips. I kissed him back. And then immediately I shoved him off of me with all my might. All six-foot-two of him went stumbling onto the other side of the boardwalk. He fell hard. I looked at him in shock for a second. I had my hands over my mouth and then, almost instantaneously, I realized what I had done, and I ran over to him. "Oh my God. Oh my God, David, are you okay?"

He laughed. He didn't seem drunk, but he must've been. I helped him up. He started walking again. He looked back at me and said, "Good night, Carm. I'm good."

I stood there watching him for what seemed like forever till he walked onto the ferry. He never turned back. Not once.

I couldn't believe what had happened. I watched the ferry as it left the dock. My mind was going a mile a minute. My boss. No, my friend. No, my fucking boss kissed me. He's not really my brother. But he kinda sorta is. Gross. But it wasn't gross. Kinda hot actually. Okay wait, that's wrong. That's so wrong! It's David. Executive. Totally out of my league. Then again, clearly NOT out of my league. No, a rich, cute White guy who could have any girl he wanted kissed ME! Oh my God! Awesome! Wait. No, he's married. Oh my God, he's MARRIED! What a jerk. Okay, but his wife, what's her name? Oh yeah, Monica. She's a super douche. Man, she'd be pissed. Maybe that's why he's looking for someone else. Anyone else. Wait, that's not good either. I'm not just anyone! Fuck! What the hell was he thinking? He's my boss! Idiot. Okay, he's not an idiot. He wasn't thinking. That's it. He wasn't thinking. My Da-veed would have never done that to me if he wasn't drunk. He'd never confuse me. He'd never hurt me. Okay. He was drunk. That's it. I can deal with that. He was drunk, he won't even remember.

Satisfied with my analysis and no longer able to see the ferry, I turned on my heels and started to walk back. I was feeling a little settled about it now and feeling grateful no one saw anything. My biggest problem was hoping he'd not even remember or, if he did, we'd just let it go. I was thinking of my strategy on how to deal with it tomorrow—if he even showed up for work.

I kept walking on the boardwalk towards Congress Street debating whether or not it was worth it to take a taxi after all. I knew it was worth it; I just didn't know if I could afford it. It was one of those weeks in between payday. And then, as I looked up, right in front of me, under the light post, standing with his arms crossed and a lit cigarette dangling from his lips, was Scot. He grabbed the cigarette from his mouth and let out a few rings. "Well, there, Carm, watchya doin'?" he said knowingly.

"Hey, um hi… Scot." Clearly I was a little startled. "Um, just walked David to the ferry…it's cold, huh?"

"Hmm. Didn't seem too cold from where I was standing." He stamped out his cigarette with his foot.

I didn't say a word.

"You know, Carm, your biggest tell that something is either wrong or going on is that you call David 'David' and not your little pet name, 'Da-veed.'" He was so proud of himself. He waited a sec. "You wanna talk about it?"

"Nope. I don't. It's no big deal. He was just a little drunk, that's all, okay? He won't even remember in the morning. Honestly, I don't even know what you're talking about."

He laughed that belly laugh and then sighed. "Well, let's just admit we both know exactly what I'm talking about. But if you don't want to talk about it, that's cool. I'm here for you if you ever change your mind."

"I know that. I do. Goodnight, Scot." I made up my mind; I hailed a cab. With Scot there, I really had no choice. Taking the train at night would have been an issue with any of the guys. I hated that it wasn't payday.

The next day was Friday and, as always, I walked around the office collecting breakfast orders. Normally I would go to my boys first, but most of them weren't in the office yet, so I started at one of the other departments and worked my way back. When I got to our area, the boys were all completely hungover. They looked bad. And the way you could tell was because it was clearly baseball cap and sunglasses day in the office. Talk about a telltale sign.

I had thought about David all night. What would I say? How would I act? Would he even remember? I wondered if he'd be mad at me for pushing him so hard. I was feeling a little bad but I was betting on him not remembering a thing, and hoping Scot would just let it go.

Finally, I got to our group of boys. For the most part, none of them wanted to order anything at all; they were sick at the thought. "James, you sure you don't want your normal bacon, egg, and cheese sandwich? Where the egg yolk just oozes all over the bread...You sure?" I said it just for kicks to see him swoon in pain. Scot seemed to be the only one with an order. Scot could drink any of them under the table and still order breakfast in the morning. He ordered his usual and gave me his cash. He asked me again, "You good?" I played like I had no idea what he was talking about. "Of course. Why wouldn't I be?" He laughed and shook his head. I smiled back and winked at him, and then walked over to David's desk.

David's head was on the table. He still had on his Red Sox baseball cap and sunglasses, but he knew I was there. "David you want breakfast? Maybe an aspirin?"

He sighed. You could feel how bad he felt. He looked up and took off his glasses, "Carm, I'm so sor—" I stopped him.

"Don't." I said quietly. I was firm and serious. I grabbed his arm and whispered in his ear. "It's cool. We're cool. And we always will be."

Bink walked by and stopped at David's desk. "Hey, what happened when I left last night? Anything good? I feel like I missed so much leaving so early. What'd you guys end up doing?"

At the same time both David and I answered emphatically, "Nothing!"

There was a moment of silence and then David myself, and Scot busted up laughing! Poor James seemed confused, as if he had somehow missed the joke, but the three of us just couldn't stop giggling. Even Edward and the rest of the guys were trying to figure out what was so funny.

That day, more than most, solidified my friendship with the boys for sure. Clearly, I had my head on straight about what happened between me and David, but I can't say I never dreamed or thought about it again. Of course I did. I was a teenage girl after all. But the truth is I was far more in love with the really cool bond I had with these yuppie boys. I trusted them so much, felt more myself around them than I ever did in the hood or even at dance rehearsals with my dance team. When I was around them, working or hanging with them, I felt the same way I did when I used to dance alone in the early mornings, out on the streets under the lamp post. I felt like I had the world's attention. I mattered. These guys, they didn't feel sorry for me. If anything, they seemed to expect so much from me. They always wanted an encore. Part of it was because they didn't know much about my past. Even if they had inklings, they didn't seem to care. They loved me anyways. And I loved them for it. David's one drunken kiss eventually became just more evidence to me of how normal I really was to them.

***

And so it was Monday morning.

It was raining. I was late and Toni—the fabulous receptionist—had set up the conference room for me and lied to Sharon that I had gone to the doctor's. Sharon was now telling me, "Everything's going to be just fine." I didn't trust her as far as I could throw her, so I knew something was up. I settled in at my desk, knowing that after the boys' meeting I could go with Scot for our regularly scheduled cigarette break and he'd tell me what was going on.

For whatever reason, the sales board had been partially covered. Normally, it tallied the boys' sales and was a visual reminder of who was "winning." I always found it interesting that they all competed with each other but were also such good friends. I learned early on that that was the nature of their business. They were salesmen. At the same time I noticed the board, I also realized there weren't that many people in the office in general. It must've been an important Monday morning strategy meeting. I really had to treat Toni to lunch or something big, because that would have been a huge disaster if coffee, muffins, note tablets, and all the other little things hadn't been set up. I would have been in big trouble!

Sharon kept smiling over at her desk, whistling at times, and I kept feeling uneasy. I pretended to ignore it, but I couldn't wait for these boys to finish their meeting. Another cool thing about my boys, if I couldn't get info out of David—who was the king of keeping secrets—I could always finagle whatever gossip I might've missed out of Bink. And if all that failed for some reason, Scot might as well have been my best girlfriend. He'd spill just for a cigarette if he'd run out. I felt satisfied I'd know soon enough what was going on, so I started on my to-do list. And then Kenneth, yes, Vice President of the company Kenneth, out of nowhere, was standing at my desk.

"Oh, hey, hi…good morning," I said, stumbling all over my words.

"Carmen, can you follow me into the conference room please?" He said it very professionally. I could see Sharon gleefully smiling at her desk. Oh God, something was really up. I was surely in trouble if Kenneth was summoning me to the conference room.

I got up immediately from my desk and followed Kenneth in. Sharon walked in behind me. The room was filled with people, standing room only. It was odd. We never had a floor meeting in the conference room, precisely because it was too small to fit everyone. All my boys were sitting around the table, with Edward at the head. Kenneth's chair was normally at the other end of the table but he motioned to me to sit down instead. I shook my head no, but Edward told me to sit down, so I made my way through a few people and sat right down. I couldn't stop fidgeting.

Edward started, "We all know why we're here…well, most of us do." There was a collective laugh. Some sort of inside joke I apparently missed. That's what I got for being late.

Toni slipped into the meeting. Now, I KNEW something was wrong! She'd put the phones on night ring, something we never did during the day unless it was an emergency.

Edward continued, "As we all know, I've had to make some decisions putting the best interests of our department, and the company as a whole, first on many occasions." He was looking straight at me. My heart sank. "Sometimes I have to make a decision that, well, I wish I didn't have to." I swallowed hard. I looked over to my right where David was sitting, and he just sat there grinning. Edward continued on. "This time, I'm happy to say, I've made a decision that is in the best interest of an individual." Everyone turned and looked at me.

I was so confused. I looked behind me to see if there was something I hadn't noticed before. Again, a collective laugh from everyone in the room.

Edward started again. "Carmen." He paused. "This is the easiest decision I've ever had to make." He paused. "I'm firing you."

I looked at him blankly. "What?" I said almost in pain. People started clapping and laughing, and I felt a little comforted that this was some sort of joke that I still wasn't getting.

Edward said it again, "Carmen, we're firing you. But we're not firing you because you've done a bad job. It's the opposite. You've done such a remarkable job that we want you to go to school. To college. And everyone in the room has decided, the company has decided, to help you do it."

One by one, each of the guys pulled out college applications from different colleges and universities and put them on the table. People that were standing around the conference room table held up the applications in their hands. I looked around the room stunned.

Edward continued on, "You're too smart. You should be in school, Carmen. And we're gonna help you get there. We have twenty two applications here. Everyone wants you to go to their alma mater. We'll help you dwindle them down to a reasonable amount to fill out. Everyone's written recommendations." He looked over at Kenneth. "And once you know what schools you might want to visit, we'll cover the cost for you to check them out." Kenneth smiled and nodded in agreement.

I was starting to understand what was happening. Toni looked over at me as if she wanted to hug me. She seemed so proud of me. I was overwhelmed. They all thought I was smart enough to go to college. Oh my God. David. He convinced them all I could go to school. Surely I'd fail. They were mistaken. I sat there dumbfounded. My chest hurt. It was starting to fill with fear.

And then I felt the hand on my shoulder again. Comfort. Security. Da-veed. My body relaxed again. I calmed down. He smiled. There were a few more words I barely heard, but I nodded up and down trying to smile. I wiped the tears from my face and kept staring at the long table filled with applications.

The meeting was over. People clapped and then one by one came over and congratulated me. They gave me their two cents as to why I should go to their college or university. It was so weird. As people left the meeting, you could hear them talking about why their college was better and the one I should go to. I was speechless. Still sitting at the table were David, James, Scot, and Edward. Toni shut the door behind her as she left.

It was silent. I kept staring at all the applications.

"Hey, Carm, you okay?" David said, still holding onto my shoulder.

"Uh huh." I sniffled. He let go.

"Carmen, this is an amazing opportunity," Bink chimed in. "You understand that, right? And we're not really firing you—though that was a nice touch, Edward. We just know you should be in school so you can be whatever you want to be." He was always over-enthusiastic and positive. I loved him.

"Uh huh." I was holding back tears as best I could.

Edward stood up. "Well, you need some time to think about all of this. But, when you're ready, we're here to help walk you through this."

Before I could say a word, Toni walked back in and motioned to David that he had to take a call. He got up from the chair and high-fived Bink as he passed on by. "She's going. And she's going to URI, Edward. It's not even a question." They all laughed. Clearly University of Rhode Island graduates.

They all walked out the door. It was just me and Scot now sitting at the conference room table. Again, silence.

"Was this your doing, Scot?"

"Yup. Well, no, mostly Dave. And Bink too. Yup."

"You want me to leave here?"

"Carm. We don't want you to leave, we want you to have more. Have more of whatever you want. You deserve more."

"You don't get it. I'm not that smart. I faked it. I won't get in. You guys think I'm so much better than I am, but I'm not school smart. I'm street smart and I must be real good cause y'all believe it. I'm telling you I won't even get in. I'm not book smart at all. And I can't afford it—"

He cut me off. "We think you're smart. We know you're smart. It's that simple."

Tears were streaming down my face now. "What if I don't get in?"

"You'll get in. Trust me. With Kenneth's recommendation alone you'll get in somewhere, if not everywhere."

There was silence again.

"I don't have the money for—"

He cut me off quicker this time. "Enough with the excuses. We'll figure it out. One thing at a time, okay?"

"Okay. But Scot, what if I get in and then quit? What if I get kicked out? Or, what if it just takes me so long because I really am dumb? And I mean, what if it takes me forever? What if I'm twenty-eight when I finally graduate? I mean, I'll be the oldest person—"

He cut me off again. He looked straight at me this time. "You know, you're right. You might fail. You might fail more than once. And maybe you will quit. But if you fall, I promise you, we'll be right here to help you back up. You're going to have to trust that, trust us." There was another patch of silence. And he started up again, "Carm, it's real simple: You can be twenty-eight years old and have graduated from college, or you can be twenty-eight years old and have never graduated at all."

His words hit me like a punch in the gut. "That's what my Mama would have said."

And without skipping a beat, he said matter-of-factly, "I know."

I couldn't help but laugh, "Scot, you're such a goof! Jeez!"

"Well, how about this—let's grab a smoke? I bet Mama Swa-ez never asked you that?"

"Sure." We both laughed out loud and started gathering the applications.

I walked back to my desk and set down the pile of applications. I was about to head downstairs to meet Scot for our scheduled cigarette break, when I looked up and noticed the sales board. It had been unveiled. The right-hand corner was a separate graph. It listed all the college applications, the corresponding alums, what portion of the application had been filled out, dates due, and what percentage of the application had to be finished. I looked around the room. I couldn't believe it. All these important people caring so much about me—of course I'd have to try. I'd have to at least try.

David walked over to my desk and hugged me hard. "You're gonna be brilliant, Carm. And you're gonna be just fine." And just like Mama, he kissed me on the forehead.

"I know," I said. "I know."

That following year, I made my way to college.

* * *

I don't know if I ever needed a dad. I think maybe it was that I needed a whole bunch of them. And I had them. In a lot of different ways.

I was never really angry with you. I didn't know you. And surely, I was never angry with Mama. I loved her so much. I'm grateful to have known her for as long as I did. Most times, I was just confused. Maybe even lonely. Sometimes, I could be in a room full of people and still be there all alone. That was hard. But it was okay.

People ask me all the time if I would have wanted to meet you—if I wanted to meet my dad. And the truth is I wouldn't change a thing.

I wish I knew Mama longer, so many of the memories keep slipping away. But I did good. And I turned out alright. I don't think I would have met such beautiful people in my life if things were different. I'm not sure I could give them up for anything in the world. They're my family.

I'm grateful I'm here. And I thank you for that. But I had a pretty good childhood and I had all the dads a kid could ever want.

I really did.

The End...actually, a new beginning.

About the Author

Carmen Lezeth Suarez was born and raised in Boston but now calls Los Angeles home. She spends most of her days trying to be better than she used to be.

To learn more about Carmen, visit her creative space:

www.carmensuarez.com

Made in the USA
San Bernardino, CA
07 June 2018